CONTRACTED AS HIS CINDERELLA BRIDE

CONTRACTED AS HIS CINDERELLA BRIDE

HEIDI RICE

MILLS & BOON

First published in Great Britain 2019
by Mills & Boon, an imprint of HarperCollins*Publishers*
1 London Bridge Street, London, SE1 9GF

Large Print edition 2019

© 2019 Heidi Rice

ISBN: 978-0-263-08306-4

MIX
Paper from
responsible sources
FSC™ C007454

This book is produced from independently certified
FSC™ paper to ensure responsible forest management. For
more information visit www.harpercollins.co.uk/green.

Printed and bound in Great Britain
by CPI Group (UK) Ltd, Croydon, CR0 4YY

To my editor Bryony—
I couldn't do this without you!

CHAPTER ONE

'CALLING RIDERS IN the vicinity of the Strand. Got a pick-up at the jeweller's Mallow and Sons. Drop-off in Bloomsbury.'

Alison Jones skidded to a stop at the amber light on Waterloo Bridge to decipher the crackle of the dispatcher's voice on her radio through the driving rain.

Cold water had seeped through her waterproof hours ago as the rush hour had slowed to a crawl in London's West End. She'd been ready to crash head-first into a bubble bath since six o'clock and lick her wounds from another evening pedalling the mean streets of Soho. But once she'd registered the instruction, she clicked on the call button and shouted into her receiver. 'Rider 524. Got it!'

She still had several instalments to pay on the debt she'd racked up four years ago for her mum's funeral—and next month's rent on her room in the house she shared with a group of other fashion students in Whitechapel wasn't going to pay itself. Plus she'd already reached peak misery for the evening. She certainly couldn't get any wetter.

The dispatcher confirmed her pick-up as she tried to focus through her exhaustion.

'Delivery's a wedding ring,' he shouted. 'Client's name for drop-off is Dominic LeGrand, address is…'

A shiver wracked Ally's body, the address barely registering as the name scraped across her consciousness, triggering a wealth of disturbing memories from the summer she had turned thirteen.

The heady scent of wild grass and roses. The baking heat of the Provence sun warming her skin. Pierre LeGrand's face—so handsome, so charming—his voice deep and paternalistic.

'Call me Papa, Alison.'

Her mother's smile, so untroubled and full of hope.

'Pierre is definitely the one, Ally. He loves me. He'll take care of us now.'

And then the pulse of heat settled low in her abdomen as she pictured Dominic. The memory of Pierre's sixteen-year-old son was as vivid and disturbing as if she'd seen him yesterday, not twelve years ago.

Those sensual lips always quirked in an insolent, *don't-give-a-damn* smile; those chocolate eyes full of resentment and secrets; the mysterious crescent-shaped scar that hooked his left eyebrow; the brutally short dark blond hair that had lightened in the sun and given his brooding beauty a golden glow.

Dominic, who had been beautiful and bad and fascinating, and landed like a fallen angel into that perfect summer bringing with him danger and excitement.

'I can't take the job,' Ally croaked into the receiver, as the memory of her final night in Provence returned, too.

Her mother's face—so sad, so fragile—a purpling bruise marring her cheekbone. The cloying scent of lavender and gin. Her mother's voice—frantic and fearful and slightly slurred.

'Something terrible's happened, baby. Pierre's very angry with me and Dominic. We have to leave.'

A bus horn blared beside her, jerking Ally out of her trance. She shoved the distressing, confusing memories back where they belonged.

When she'd buried her mother four years ago, she'd finally stopped reliving the horror of that night as she stood over the grave and felt nothing but relief that Monica Jones was finally at peace.

She couldn't take this job. She didn't want to see Dominic LeGrand again. Especially as Dominic wasn't the reckless, delinquent boy who had starred in all those innocent adolescent fantasies a lifetime ago, but a billionaire property developer now. Hadn't the tabloids dubbed him 'Love-Rat LeGrand' a year ago after one of his supermodel girlfriends had sold her story of their affair for a six-figure sum? The wedding ring had to be for the fairy-tale romance with Mira Somebody Ally had read about a month ago.

'What do you mean you're not taking the job? I just put it through the system.' The dispatcher's voice sliced into Ally's misery. 'Either you do it or I'm pulling you from the roster. Make up your mind.'

Ally breathed in and breathed out, trying to control the panic making the air clog in her lungs.

She *had* to take this job. She didn't have a

choice. She couldn't afford to lose the work. Pressing her freezing finger on the radio, she spoke into the receiver. 'Okay, I'll take it. Give me that address again.'

'The wedding's off, Mira. Your hook-up with Andre the ski instructor has seen to that.' Dominic LeGrand kept his voice even; he wasn't sad or upset, he was furious. They'd had a deal. And his so-called fiancée had broken it.

'But I... I told you it was nothing, Dominic.' Tears sheened Mira's eyes, her voice breaking with emotion. Dominic's impatience sharpened his fury. The woman had the emotional maturity of a two-year-old.

'I thought I made it plain before we entered into this arrangement I expected exclusivity. I'm not marrying a woman I can't trust.'

'But I didn't sleep with Andre... I swear,' Mira said. 'I was a little drunk and flirtatious, that was all.' She leaned across his desk, her breasts pressing provocatively against her low-cut gown, her lips pursed into the pout he'd found hot two months ago, when they'd first met. 'I'm not going to lie—I quite like that you're a little jealous,' she added.

The coy flirtatious look on her face was probably supposed to be enticing. It wasn't.

'I'm not jealous, Mira. I'm angry. It's a breach of our agreement. It could jeopardise the Waterfront deal.' Which was the only reason he'd asked her to marry him in the first place.

The Jedah Consortium, who owned the tract of real estate in Brooklyn he wanted to develop, was made up of conservative businessmen from a string of oil-rich Middle Eastern countries. They'd been wary of doing business with him after Catherine Zalinski's kiss-and-tell article last year had made him look like a man who couldn't control his own libido, let alone the women in his life.

This marriage was supposed to fix that, until pictures of his fiancée kissing her ski instructor had hit the tabloids this afternoon.

'The whole purpose of this marriage was to stop any more unsavoury gossip about my private life,' he added, in case she didn't get it.

'But you left me alone for a whole month.' The pout became more pronounced. 'I waited for you to come to Klosters but you didn't. We haven't slept together in even longer. What did you expect me to do?'

He hadn't had time to go all the way to Klosters to visit her. The fact he hadn't been particularly desperate to ease the sexual drought confirmed something else—this agreement had been ill-advised from the start. He'd grown bored of Mira even sooner than he'd expected, in bed as well as out of it.

'I expected you to keep your mouth off other men. And your legs closed.'

'Dominic, don't say things like that.' The shocked hurt in her eyes looked genuine. Almost. 'It makes me feel cheap.'

He let his gaze coast down the designer dress he'd paid for.

'Mira, the one thing you're not is cheap,' he said wryly.

She stiffened at the insult.

'Find your own way out,' he said. 'We're done here.'

'You… You heartless bastard.'

Mira's hand whipped out so fast, he heard the crack before the pain blazed across his cheekbone.

He leapt out of his chair, holding her wrist before she could strike him again. But the smarting pain where she'd struck him had a bitter memory spinning back of another slap, from the summer he'd finally been invited into his father's world—only to be kicked out again a month later—and the voice of the girl who had defended him.

'You mustn't hit Dominic, you'll hurt him, Papa.'

'Some people deserve to be hurt, ma petite.*'*

'You're right, Mira, I *am* heartless. I'm also a bastard.' He ground out the words, the hollow ache in his chest at the memory of that slap an emotion he'd thought he'd cauterised long ago. How infuriating to find he hadn't…quite. 'I consider that a strength,' he added, releasing Mira's wrist. 'Now get out. Before I have you arrested for assault.'

Mira's face collapsed, her lips trembling. 'I hate you.'

So what? he thought dispassionately, as she swung round and rushed out of his study.

Hearing the front door slam, he walked to the drinks cabinet, swiped the trickle of blood at the corner of his mouth, then poured himself a glass of single malt Scotch.

He only had a week to find himself another wife to secure the deal he needed to take his business to the next level. The business he'd built from nothing after crawling off his father's estate that summer, his ribs feeling as if they were being crushed in a vice, the welts on his back burning.

He'd flagged down a truck, and the driver had taken pity on him, giving him a ride all the way to Paris. As he'd sunk in and out of consciousness on that endless, agonising journey, he had promised himself he would never see or speak to his father again. And that he would build something to prove to his father, and everyone else who had rejected him, had belittled or dismissed him, that they were wrong.

He welcomed the sting as the liquor hit his split lip.

He would find another wife. Preferably one who did exactly what he told her and knew how to keep her legs closed. But tonight he planned to celebrate a lucky escape.

CHAPTER TWO

'GET OUT OF my way, you filthy…' The woman's voice trailed off into a sneer as she shoved Ally and her bike out of the way.

Ally stumbled, rammed into the gatepost, the bike's pedal scrapping against her calf as the woman marched past her and got into a sleek red sports car.

Ally hauled the bike up. She would have shouted after the woman, but she was too tired and too anxious to bother—and anyway the woman wouldn't have heard her in the rain.

The car peeled away from the kerb in a squeal of rubber.

Ally watched the red tail lights disappear round the corner of the Georgian garden square.

Hadn't that been Mira Whatshername? The woman the wedding ring she had in her pack was for?

The woman had looked furious. Maybe there

was trouble in paradise? Ally pushed the thought to one side.

So not your business.

She wheeled the bike to the back of the mansion house, which stood at the end of the square in its own grounds. Taking a fortifying breath, she propped the bike against the back wall and pressed her freezing finger into the brass bell at the trade entrance.

He won't answer the door. He'll have staff to do it. Stop freaking out.

The rain had reached monsoon levels as she'd left Mallow and Sons. It beat down on her now, drenching her. The tiny package she'd collected weighed several tons in the bike bag hooked over her back.

Unfortunately the freezing March rain, and the numbness in all her extremities, not to mention the now throbbing ache in her calf muscle, felt like the least of her worries as the harsh memories continued to mess with her head.

Stepping back from the door, she peered up at the house. Every window was dark, bar one on the floor above. Swallowing heavily, she pressed the bell again, with a bit more conviction. A figure appeared at the window. Tall and broad and indistinct through the deluge. Her heartbeat clattered into her throat.

It's not him, it's not him, it's not him.

The pep talk became a frantic prayer as she detected the sound of footsteps inside the house.

She jerked her bag to her front. She should get the wedding ring out so she could hand it over as soon as the door opened.

She fumbled with the wet fastenings, her heartbeat getting so loud it drowned out the sound of the storm.

A light in the hallway snapped on, casting a yellow glow over the rain-slicked panels, then a large silhouette filled the bevelled glass.

Ally barely had a chance to brace herself before the door swung wide. A tall man filled the space, his face thrown into shadow by the light from the hallway. But Ally's numbed fingers seized on the bike bag when he spoke—his deep, even voice thrusting a knife into the memories lurking in her belly like malevolent beasts.

'Bonsoir.'

The French accent rippled over her skin, sending sickening shivers of heat through her chilled body—and making the ball of shame wedged in her solar plexus swell.

How could he still have the power to do that? When she was a grown woman now, not an impressionable teenager in the throes of puberty?

'You'd better come inside before you drown,' he murmured, standing aside to hold the door open.

The manoeuvre lit the harsh planes and angles of his face. Ally stood locked in place absorbing the face she had once spent hours fantasising about.

Dominic had always been striking, but maturity had turned his boyish masculine beauty into something so intense it was devastating.

The blond buzz cut had darkened into a tawny brown streaked with gold, and was long enough now to curl around the collar of his shirt. Those dark chocolate eyes had no laughter lines yet, but then that would have been a contradiction in terms—because the Dominic she remembered had never laughed. A new bump on the bridge of his nose joined the old scar on his brow, while the shadow of stubble marked him out as a man now instead of a boy.

As Ally's gaze devoured the changes, she registered how much more jaded the too-old look in his eyes had become, and how much more ruthless the cynical curve of those sensual lips.

The inappropriate shivers turned into seismic waves.

'*Vite, garçon*, before we *both* drown.' The snapped command made her realise she'd been staring.

She forced herself to walk past him into the hallway.

Just give him the ring, then this nightmare will be over.

She bent to fumble with her bike bag, wishing she hadn't removed her helmet, but luckily he didn't seem to be looking at her. He had called her a boy, after all.

The drip, drip, drip of the rain coming off her waterproof seemed deafening in the silent hallway as he closed the door.

'You're a girl,' he murmured.

She made the mistake of looking round.

His scarred brow lifted as the chocolate gaze glided over her figure, making the growled acknowledgement disturbingly intimate.

'I'm a woman,' she said. 'Is that a problem?'

'*Non.*' His lips lifted on one side. The cynical half-smile reminded her so forcefully of the boy, she had to stifle a gasp. 'Do I know you?' he asked. 'You look familiar.'

'No,' she said, but the denial came out on a rasp of panic as her hand closed over the jeweller's bag.

Please don't let him recognise me—it will only make this worse.

She yanked the bag out and thrust it towards him. 'Your delivery, Mr LeGrand.'

She kept her head bent as he took the package, snatching her hand away as warm fingertips brushed her palm and the buzz of reaction zipped up her arm.

'You're shivering. Stay and dry off.' It sounded more like a demand than a suggestion, but she shook her head.

'I'm fine,' she said, drawing out her data console. 'Sign in the box,' she added, trying for efficient and impersonal, and getting breathless instead.

He tucked the jeweller's bag under his arm and took the data-recording device, brushing her hand again.

'You're freezing,' he said, sounding annoyed now and impatient. 'You should stay until the storm passes.' He signed his name and handed the device back. 'It's the least I can do after dragging you out in this weather on a fool's errand.'

'A fool's errand? How?' she asked, then wanted to bite off her tongue.

Shut up, Ally, why did you ask him that?

Starting a conversation was the last thing she needed to do. Her heart thumped her chest wall so hard she was amazed she didn't pass out. To her surprise, though, he answered her.

'A fool's errand because I broke off the engagement approximately ten minutes ago...' The cynical tone reminded her again of the boy.

No wonder Mira Something had been furious. She'd just been dumped.

He ripped open the package and drew out the velvet jeweller's box, then flipped it open.

Ally's heart stuttered. The ring was exquisite—a platinum and gold band.

The irony washed through her, as she thought of another ring.

The ring her mother had said his father had offered her all through the summer. A dream that had died that terrible night when Pierre LeGrand had kicked them out, but the loss of which had tortured her mother for the rest of her life.

'Pierre was the only man who ever really loved me and I ruined it all, baby.'

Her mother had blamed herself, but what had she done to make Pierre so angry?

Dominic snapped the ring box closed, dragging Ally back to the present. 'Which makes this a rather expensive waste of money.'

'I'm sorry,' she mumbled, trying to swallow down the volatile emotions starting to choke her. Emotions she didn't want to examine too closely.

'Don't be,' he said. 'The engagement was a mistake. The eighty grand I spent on this ring is collateral damage.'

The offhand remark had the shame and guilt twisting in her gut.

She shoved her data device back into the pocket on her bike bag, her fingers trembling with the effort it was taking to hold back the raw emotions.

What was happening to her? Why was she making this into a big thing, when it really wasn't? Not any more. Her mother was dead, and so was Pierre. It was all ancient history now.

'I should go. I've got other jobs to get to,' she said. She just wanted to leave. To forget again. It was too painful to go over all those memories. To remember how bright and vivacious her mother had been that summer, and the hollow shell she had become after it.

'Come in and have a drink, warm up,' he said, or rather demanded.

Was he coming on to her? The thought wasn't as horrific as it should have been, which had the knot of shame in her stomach tightening. But then the clammy feel of the soaked and grubby fabric sticking to her skin made her aware of how much like a drowned rat she must look.

This man dated supermodels and heiresses— women with style and grace and effortless sex appeal. Something she had never possessed, even when she hadn't spent the last six hours cycling around London's West End in a monsoon.

'And we can deal with your leg,' he added.

'What?' she mumbled.

'Your leg.' The chocolate gaze dipped. 'It's bleeding.'

She glanced down to see blood seeping out

of a gash on her calf, exposed by a rip in her leggings. It must have been caused by her altercation with his fiancée—or rather his ex-fiancée—and she'd been too cold to feel it.

'It's nothing,' she said. 'I have to go.'

But as she turned to leave, he spoke again.

'*Arrêtes*. It's *not* nothing. It's bleeding. It could get infected. You're not going out there until it has been cleaned.'

The emotion started to choke her. She couldn't stay, couldn't accept his kindness—however brusque and domineering.

'I've got work, another job,' she added, frantically. 'I can't stay.'

'I'll pay for your time, damn it, if the problem is money. I don't want an injured cycle messenger on my conscience as well as an eighty-grand ring.'

He was too close, surrounding her in a cloud of spicy cologne and the sweet subtle whiff of whisky. Her pulse points buzzed and throbbed in an erratic rhythm.

But then he hooked a knuckle under her chin, and nudged her chin up.

'Wait a minute. I *do* know you.' His eyes narrowed as he studied her face. For the first time, he was actually seeing her. The intensity of his gaze set off bonfires of sensation all over her chilled skin. She fumbled with the helmet she had hooked over her other arm, desperate to put it on, to stop him recognising her.

But it was too late as the swift spike of memory crossed his face.

'*Monique?*' he murmured.

Tears stung her eyes. 'I'm not Monica. Monica's dead. I'm her daughter.'

'Allycat?' he said, looking as stunned as she felt.

Allycat.

The nickname reverberated in her head, the one he'd given her all those years ago. The name she had been so proud of. Once.

As if he'd flipped a switch, the adrenaline she'd been running on ever since she'd got the commission drained away, until all that was left was the shame, and anxiety. And the inappropriate heat.

She dragged in tortured breaths, struggling to contain the choking sob rising up her torso. She didn't have the strength to resist him any more. And what would be the point, anyway?

'Breathe, Allycat,' he murmured.

She gulped in air, trying to steady herself, and got a lungful of his scent—spiced with pine and soap.

'Bad night?'

'The worst.' She bit back the harsh laugh at his sanguine tone. And shuddered, the pain in her ribs excruciating as she struggled to hold the sobs at bay.

What exactly are you so upset about? Having Dominic LeGrand pity you isn't the worst thing that's ever happened to you.

'I know the feeling,' he said, the wry smile only making him look more handsome—and more utterly unattainable.

She forced a smile to her lips as she shifted away from him, and scooped up the helmet that had clattered to the floor.

'It was nice seeing you again, Dominic,' she said, although nothing could have been further from the truth. *Nice* had never been a word to describe Dominic LeGrand. 'I really do have to go now, though.'

But as she headed for the door, he stepped in front of her. 'Don't go, Allycat. Come in and dry off and clean up your leg. My offer still stands.'

She lifted her head, forced herself to meet his gaze. But where she'd expected pity, or impatience, all she saw was a pragmatic intensity—as if he were trying to see into her soul. And something else, something she didn't recognise or understand—because it almost looked like desire. But that couldn't be true.

'I can't stay,' she said, hating the tremble in her voice.

She didn't want to feel this weak, this fragile. She hated showing him even an ounce of her vulnerability, because it made her feel even more pathetic.

'Yes, you can.' He didn't budge. 'As I said, I will pay for your time,' he added, the tone rigid with purpose.

'I don't need you to do that. I'm shattered anyway. I'm just going to cycle home.' She needed to leave, before the foolish yearning to stay, and have him care for her, got the better of her.

Mon Dieu, who would have thought that Monique's shy and sheltered daughter would grow into a woman as striking and valiant as Jeanne D'Arc?

'So there are no more jobs tonight?' Dominic asked.

The girl frowned, but, even caught in the lie, her gaze remained direct. 'No, there aren't,' she said, the unapologetic tone equally captivating. 'I lied.'

He let out a rough chuckle. '*Touché*, Allycat.'

He let his gaze wander over the slim coltish figure, vibrating with tension. Her high firm breasts, outlined by her damp cycle gear, rose and fell with her staggered breaths. With her wet hair tied back in a short ponytail, damp chestnut curls clinging to the pale, almost translucent skin of her cheeks, blue-tinged shadows under her eyes, and an oil mark on her chin, she should have looked a mess. But instead she looked like the Maid of Orleans—passionate and determined.

And all the more beautiful for it.

Not unlike her mother. Or what he could remember of her mother.

Monica Jones had been his father's mistress, during that brief summer when his father had acknowledged him. But the truth was it was her daughter, the girl who stood before him now, her wide guileless eyes direct and unbowed despite her obvious misery, whom he remembered with a great deal more clarity.

She'd been a child that summer, ten or eleven maybe, but he still remembered how she had followed him around like a doting puppy. And defended him against his father's abuse. She had stood up to that bastard on his behalf, and because of that he'd felt a strange connection with her. And it seemed that connection hadn't died. Not completely.

Although it had morphed into something a great deal more potent—if the sensation that had zapped up his arm when he had touched her was anything to go by.

She was quite stunning, pure and unsullied—despite her bedraggled appearance. The compulsion to capture her cold cheeks in his palms and warm her unpainted lips with a kiss surprised him, though.

Why should he want her, when she was so unsophisticated? *Un garçon manqué.* A tomboy without an ounce of glamour or allure. Why should he care if she was cold, or wet, or injured? She wasn't his responsibility.

Perhaps it was simply the shock of seeing her again, and the memories she evoked? Maybe it was the compelling contrast she made with the woman he'd just kicked out of his life? Not spoilt, entitled and indulged but fierce and fearless and proud. The most likely explanation, though, for his attraction was that erotic spark that had arched between them the minute she'd stepped into the house.

After all, it had been over a month since he'd made love to a woman, and considerably longer since he'd felt that visceral tug of desire this woman seemed to evoke simply by breathing.

'Then I will order a car to take you and the bike home in due course,' he answered, because he was damned if he'd let her leave before he had at least had a chance to explore why she intrigued him so much. And no way was he letting her cycle home tonight. It was practically a hurricane out there.

A shiver ran through her and he noticed the small puddle forming at her feet.

'There's a bathroom on the first floor. Dry off and help yourself to the clothes in the dresser,' he said. 'I will meet you up there once I have found some medical supplies for that leg.'

The flush on her face brightened. She looked

wary and tense, like a feral kitten scared to trust a helping hand.

'You don't have to do that,' she said.

'I know,' he replied. 'Now go. *Vite.*' He shooed her upstairs. 'Before you flood my hallway.'

CHAPTER THREE

'I DISCOVERED WHERE my housekeeper hides the medical supplies,' Ally's host announced as he strolled into the large study on the first floor and placed a red box on the mahogany desk.

Ally swallowed down the lump of anxiety in her throat. She wrapped her arms around her midriff, but remained rooted to her spot by the room's large mullioned windows.

How did Dominic have the ability to suck all the oxygen out of the room simply by walking into it?

At least she was warm and clean and dry now. Unfortunately, the oversized sweatpants and top that smelled of him, which she'd found in the guest bedroom next door—after taking the world's fastest shower in the en-suite wet room—still put her at a huge disadvantage.

In her bare feet, he towered over her, his suit trousers and white shirt perfectly tailored to accentuate his lean, well-muscled body.

'I see you found some dry clothes.' He studied her makeshift outfit in a way that made her feel like a street urchin playing dress-up before a king.

The intense look had her heart thundering harder against her ribs.

'Yes, thank you,' she said.

'Is the leg still bleeding?' The gruff question had goosebumps springing up all over her skin, despite the cosy cotton sweats.

'I don't think so,' she said. 'I took a shower to clean it. I'm sure it's fine.'

'We'll see,' he said, sounding doubtful. He beckoned her with one finger and indicated a large armchair in the corner of the room. 'Sit down so I can inspect it.'

She debated arguing with him again, because goosebumps were rising on the goosebumps now at the thought of getting any closer to him. But she could see by the muscle twitching in his jaw he wasn't going to take no for an answer.

She crossed the room, trying not to limp, and sat in the chair. The sooner they got this over with, the sooner she could start breathing freely again.

To her astonishment he knelt down in front of her. She braced her hands on the arms of the chair as he opened the box, and began to rummage through the array of medical supplies.

How had this happened? How had she ended up playing doctor with Dominic LeGrand? In his billion-pound house? In the intimacy of his study? While wearing his sweats with virtually nothing under them?

The traitorous heat—which had been lodged in her belly ever since the dispatcher had said his name—throbbed and glowed at her core.

But this time, she replayed the pep talk she'd given herself in the shower.

Why should she feel ashamed of her reaction to him? They were both consenting adults. Dominic had always captivated her, even as a delinquent boy, and he was a world-renowned womaniser now. So she was bound to find him a little overwhelming—especially as she was so pathetically inexperienced with men.

Looking after her mother and keeping food on the table and a roof over both their heads hadn't left her any time to date while she was at school. And after her mother died, trying to realise her dream of becoming a fashion designer and stop her finances from slipping into a black hole hadn't increased her opportunities much. In fact, despite a few fumbling encounters, she was still a virgin. Which explained why she had such a violent reaction to someone as overwhelming as Dominic Le-Grand.

Having rationalised her attraction, she watched him unobserved as he arranged a bandage and a packet of antiseptic wipes on the side table.

Even when he was on his knees, his head was almost level with hers. The light from the lamp behind her caught the streaks of gold in his tawny hair. She could make out the scar on his brow, the one she'd wondered about often when they were children. How had he got it?

His shoulders flexed, stretching the seams of his shirt, as he reached down to cradle her heel in his palm.

She jumped, sensation sprinting up her leg and sinking deep into her sex as callused fingers gripped her ankle.

'Does that hurt?' he asked, his chocolate gaze locking on her face.

'No, it's just…' *No man has ever touched me there before.* 'I was just surprised.' *Who knew my ankle was an erogenous zone?*

'Okay.' He frowned, but seemed to take the explanation at face value. 'Let me know if it does hurt.'

She nodded, her whole foot humming as he gripped her heel and used his other hand to lift the leg of her sweatpants past her knee.

He hissed as the gash was revealed. It wasn't too deep, more like a bad scrape where the pedal had dug into the skin, but it was still bleeding a little and there was some bruising visible around the wound.

'Nasty,' he murmured as he grabbed one of the antiseptic wipes with his free hand.

He ripped the small packet open with his teeth.

'Do you know how you did it?' he asked, dabbing at the wound.

'I got in the way of your fiancée while she was leaving,' she said.

His fingers tensed on her heel. 'Mira did this?' he said and she could hear the fury in his voice.

She nodded, wishing she could take the words back.

Why did you bring up his broken engagement?

He'd seemed pragmatic about it downstairs, but how did she know that wasn't all an act? Like the act he had put on as a boy, when his father had referred to him as 'my bastard son' at the supper table, or the *don't-give-a-damn* smile he'd sent her when she had witnessed Pierre backhand him across the face—and she'd tried to defend him.

'Some people deserve to be hurt, ma petite.*'*

His father's answer still haunted her.

No one deserved to be hurt, least of all Dominic, who had seemed to her back then— despite that *don't-give-a-damn* bravado—like a lost boy, jealously guarding secrets he refused to share.

What if he was just as hurt about his broken engagement? And his anger now was only there to disguise that hurt?

'I'm sorry,' she said. 'I didn't mean to upset you.'

'Upset me?' The flash of anger was replaced

by an incredulous look. 'What could you have done to upset me?'

'By bringing up the end of your engagement. I didn't mean to remind you of it. I'm sure it must be awful for you. The break-up?'

She was babbling, but she couldn't help it, because he had settled back onto his heels and was staring at her as if she'd lost her mind.

'Alison,' he said and she could hear the hint of condescension. 'In the first place, *you* haven't upset me. *She* has, by her spoilt, unpleasant be-haviour. She made you bleed…'

'I'm sure it was an accident,' she said, despite the warm glow at his concern.

'Knowing Mira and her selfish, capricious temperament, I doubt that,' he said. 'And in the second place, the break-up has not upset me. The engagement was a mistake and the mar-riage would have been an even bigger one.'

'But you must have loved her once?' she said, then felt like a fool, when the rueful smile wid-ened.

'Must I?' he said. 'Why must I?'

'Because… Because you were going to marry her?' *Wasn't it obvious?*

He tilted his head, and studied her. 'I see

you're still as much of a romantic as you were at ten,' he said, with much more than just a hint of condescension.

'I wasn't ten that summer, I was thirteen,' she countered.

'Really?' he said, mocking her now. 'So grown up.'

She shifted in her seat, supremely uncomfortable. It was as if he could see right past the bravado, the pretence of maturity, to the girl she'd been all those years ago when she'd idolised him. But she wasn't that teenager any more, she was twenty-five years old. And maybe she didn't have much relationship experience, but she had enough life experience to make up for it.

'If I was a romantic then,' she said, because maybe she had been, 'I'm certainly not one now.'

'Then why would you believe I was in love with Mira?' he said, as if it were the most ridiculous thing in the world.

'Maybe because you were planning to spend the rest of your life with her.' She wanted to add a 'Duh' but managed to control it. The room was already full to bursting with sarcasm.

'It wasn't a love match,' he said, the pragmatic tone disconcerting as he bent his head and continued tending her leg as he spoke. 'I needed a wife to secure an important business deal and Mira fit the bill. Or so I thought. But even if I hadn't discovered my mistake in time, the marriage was only supposed to last for a few months.'

'Your marriage had a sell-by date?' she asked, shocked by the depth of his cynicism.

'I might have been misguided enough to propose to Mira,' he said, smiling at her as he grabbed the bandage on the side table. 'But I would never be foolish enough to shackle myself to her, or any woman, for life.'

'I see,' she said, although she really didn't.

He'd always been guarded, and wary, even at sixteen. But had he always been this jaded?

One encounter blasted into her brain, when she'd caught him sitting in one of the chateau's walled gardens, inhaling deeply on a cigarette after his father had goaded him at the lunch table, calling him a name in French she hadn't really understood but had known was bad.

'You shouldn't smoke. It's bad for you. Papa will be angry.'

'Go ahead and tell him if you want, Allycat. He won't care.'

He'd had the same mocking smile on his face then as he had now, but she'd seen the sadness in his eyes—and had known his father's insult had hurt him much more than he'd been letting on. There was no sadness in his eyes now, though, just a sort of rueful amusement at her naiveté.

He finished bandaging her leg.

'All done.' He ran his thumbs along her calf, and she shivered as a trail of fire was left by the light caress. 'How does it feel?'

'Good,' she said and then flushed at his husky chuckle.

Had he sensed it wasn't only her leg she was talking about?

A sensual smile curved his lips and her breath clogged in her lungs.

Yes, he did know.

'Bien,' he murmured, then grabbed the arms of the chair, caging her in for a moment as he levered himself to his feet.

Her heartbeat thundered into her throat and some other key parts of her anatomy as he offered her his hand.

'Let's try walking on it,' he said.

She placed her fingers in his palm, but as she got to her feet the warm grip had the sweet spot between her thighs becoming heavy and hot.

She tested her leg as he led her across the room.

'Still good?' he asked, still smiling that knowing smile.

'Yes,' she said. 'Still good.' And couldn't resist smiling back at him.

Maybe it was dangerous to flirt with him—if that was what they were doing. But she'd never had much of a chance to flirt with anyone before. And certainly not someone as gorgeous as he was.

And let's not forget the massive crush you had on him once upon a time, her subconscious added, helpfully.

'How about that drink?' he asked as he let her hand go, to walk to the liquor cabinet in the bookshelves.

She ought to say no. But she was feeling languid and a little giddy. Maybe it was the fire crackling in the hearth, or the sound of the rain still beating down outside, or the cosy feel of the sweats she'd borrowed, or the glimmer of appreciation in his hot chocolate eyes—which was probably all in her imagination. Or maybe it was the fact he had tended her leg.

When was the last time anyone had taken care of her?

Whatever the reason, she couldn't seem to conjure the ability to be careful or cautious for once. She'd denied herself so many things in the last twelve years—why should she deny herself a chance to have a drink with a man who had always fascinated her?

'Were you serious about ordering me a cab home?' she asked. Because she couldn't drink if she was going to have to cycle all the way to East London.

'Of course,' he said.

'Then thank you, I'd love a drink.'

'What would you like? I have whisky. Gin. Brandy.' He opened the drinks cabinet and bent to look inside, giving her a far too tempting view of tight male buns confined in designer trousers. 'A spicy Merlot? A refreshing Chablis?'

'Spoken like a true Frenchman,' she teased.

'*C'est vrai.* I am French. I take my wine seriously,' he said, laying on his accent extra thick and making her grin.

'The Merlot sounds good,' she said.

He poured the red wine into a crystal tumbler, his fingers brushing hers as he passed her the glass. The prickle of reaction sprinted up her arm, but it didn't scare her or shame her this time. It excited her.

She took a sip of the wine, and the rich fruity flavours burst on her tongue.

'Bon?' he asked.

'Very.'

He leaned his hips against the cabinet and crossed his arms over his chest, making his pectoral muscles flex distractingly against the white linen.

'You're not drinking?' she asked.

'I have already had one whisky tonight. And I want to keep a clear head.'

'Oh?' she said. She wanted to ask why he needed to keep a clear head, but it seemed like a loaded question—especially when he smiled that sensual smile again, as if they were sharing an intimate secret.

She got a little distracted by the astonishing beauty of his face—rugged and masculine—

dappled by firelight and the ridged contours of his chest visible through the tailored shirt.

She took another sip of the wine, let the warmth of it spread through her torso. This was definitely better than having to cycle back to Whitechapel in the pouring rain.

Mira Whatsherface's loss was Ally Jones's gain.

'Are you enjoying the view?' The deep mocking voice had her gaze jerking back to his face.

She blinked, blinded by the heat of his smile. Momentarily.

Her cheeks heated.

For goodness' sake, Ally, stop staring at his exceptional chest and make some small talk.

'What's the deal?' she asked.

His scarred eyebrow arched. 'Deal?'

'The deal you were prepared to enter into a loveless short-term marriage for,' she elaborated.

'An extremely important one for my business,' he said, without an ounce of embarrassment or remorse. 'There is a large tract of undeveloped land on the Brooklyn waterfront. It is the only undeveloped parcel of that size in the five boroughs. I intend to reclaim it, and build on it. Homes mostly. Unfortunately it is owned by a group of men who refuse to invest with someone they regard as—how did they put it? "Morally suspect."' He used finger quotes while sending her a wry smile. 'My private life needs to be stable and settled without a whiff of scandal while the project is in its early stages. As soon as I was in a position to engineer a board takeover and buy them out, I planned to end the marriage.'

'So it's all about money?' she said.

His smile quirked as if she had said something particularly amusing. 'Money is important. You of all people should understand that,' he said, and she felt her blush heat. 'But no, it's not all about money. This is about taking my business to the next level. This project will put LeGrand Nationale in a position to dominate the regeneration market in the United States.'

So it wasn't just about money, it was also about legacy and prestige. Was it any surprise that would be so important to him? When he had been forced to prove himself from a young age, the illegitimate son who had been called a 'bastard' by his own father. She couldn't blame him for his drive and ambition, even though his cynicism made her feel sad.

'But let's not talk about business,' he murmured as he released his arms and walked towards her. His thumb glided down her cheek and her breath caught in her throat, the sizzle of heat darting into her sex. 'Tell me about you. How did you come to be a bike messenger? Has your life been hard, since that summer, Allycat?'

His voice caressed the childhood nickname in a way that inflamed her senses—but his attention was even more potent. She needed to be careful; this was a casual conversation, nothing more.

'Not that hard,' she lied. 'I became a bike courier because it's good money. And I can fit it around my classes. I'm… I'm in college at the moment,' she added, as she found herself staring into his eyes, spotting the strands of gold in the chocolate brown.

'So you are smart as well as beautiful.' His thumb glided across her lips and her mouth opened instinctively on a sigh, the blood rushing in her ears.

'If I asked to kiss you, Alison,' he said, the

rasp of need in his voice both raw and sublime, 'what would you say?'

She nodded without thinking.

Kissing Dominic probably wasn't a good idea, but she was incapable of controlling the euphoria rioting in her blood. The knowledge he wanted her was even more intoxicating than his fresh woodsy scent and the feel of his thumb tracing over the pulse in her neck.

'You must say the word,' he coaxed as he stroked the well of her collarbone.

'Yes.' *Please.*

'Merci.'

The hoarse thank-you was as tortured as the need twisting her belly into tight knots.

Her bottom bumped the wall as he pressed her against it, found the hem of her sweatshirt and slid his hands under it to hold her steady.

Then his lips were on hers, hot and firm and seeking. A groan escaped from her constricted throat and his tongue plunged deep into her mouth.

He explored in masterful, demanding strokes as his fingers dipped beneath the waistband of her sweatpants and cupped her naked bottom.

He ripped his mouth away. 'No panties?' he

said, the pupils so dilated his chocolate brown eyes had become black.

'They… They were wet,' she choked out.

'I may have to punish you for that, Alison,' he murmured, the mocking tone so fierce it was only half joking.

Raw need careered through her.

'I want to see more of you,' he said. *'D'accord?'*

She nodded again, having lost the power of speech.

Lifting the hem of her sweatshirt, he tugged it over her head. She shuddered as his gaze glided over the damp sports bra she had donned after her shower.

Could she have been wearing anything less alluring?

But his gaze when it met hers still blazed with arousal. *'Trés belle.'*

Capturing both her wrists in one hand, he lifted her arms above her head, until she was pinned against the wall, her breasts thrust out, begging for attention, her breathing so ragged it sounded deafening.

He covered one straining breast with his free hand and scooped it free of her bra. Exposing her to his gaze.

'*Magnifique...*' he murmured, then lowered his head and licked across the swollen tip.

She bucked against his hold, shocked by the sensations firing down to her core as he teased and tortured the oversensitive peak with his tongue, his teeth.

She couldn't stop shaking, sobbing. Until he covered the erect nipple with his mouth and suckled.

It was too much and yet not nearly enough. The jut of his erection, so hard and large confined in the suit trousers, pressed against her belly. She wanted to feel it inside her, to take the ache away.

Her breathing guttered out when at last he released her engorged nipple. But the relief was short-lived, as he unhooked the bra and freed her other breast to begin again. Torturing, teasing, tormenting.

She was begging, bucking against his hold when he finally returned his mouth to hers. He held her captive, both wrists shackled above her head. The huge erection notched between her thighs, her bare breasts crushed against his chest. The hard shaft found that sweet spot through their clothing, rubbing, rocking, the waves of sensation building from her core.

The orgasm built so swiftly, she couldn't control it, the shattering wave crashing over her with staggering intensity. Her body arched as the bright light fired from her core and shattered into a million glittering shards.

She was struggling to breathe, her body slumped against his, when his voice rasped against her ear.

'*Dieu*, did you just climax, Alison?'

Her eyelids fluttered open, to find him staring at her with a need so fierce it was terrifying and liberating all at once.

Her thundering heart began to slow. He did not look happy. In fact, he looked stunned. Had she done something wrong?

'Yes…' she said. 'I'm… I'm sorry, I couldn't stop it. Was I supposed to?'

His lips quirked and then, to her astonishment, he dropped his head back and laughed.

She tugged on her arms, tried to wrestle herself free of his hold, humiliation engulfing her.

He was still fully dressed. With her bra hanging from one arm and her nipples raw and swollen where he'd played with them she'd never felt more exposed.

'I should go,' she murmured.

But he didn't release her, as the rough chuckles died. His thumbs pressed into the rampaging pulse at her wrists.

'No way. We're not finished yet. Even if you jumped the gun.'

'I said I was sorry about…' She tried to protest, but he silenced her, the swift kiss both demanding and possessive.

'There was no need to apologise,' he said, his gaze compelling—the humour replaced with something much more potent. 'Do you have any idea how adorable you are?'

The gruff words were quietly spoken, but so achingly sincere her heart punched her ribs.

Cupping her cheek, he swept his gaze over her, the approval she saw making her heartbeat thunder in her ears.

What was happening? Because this felt *too* intimate, *too* emotional. More than sex.

'Please, I…' she began.

'Shh…' He stroked his hand down to her collarbone, the ripple of sensation making her shiver. 'I wish to take you to bed, Alison. How do you feel about that?'

'I… I want you too.' *Very much.*

'Bien.'

He sent her a devilish grin, full of wickedness and intent. Letting her arms drop, he dragged the bra away, leaving her standing before him in only the baggy sweatpants.

'Très, très belle,' he murmured again, his voice thick with arousal. 'My gym pants have never looked so good.'

She crossed her arms over her breasts, brutally aware of how naked she was, compared to him.

But then he scooped her into his arms.

She grasped his neck as he marched her into the spare bedroom. The room was luxuriously furnished with a large tester bed complemented by an array of antique pieces. He closed the door to the study, so the only light in the room came from the bathroom and the bay window that looked out onto the house's grounds. The low lighting had a little of her anxiety retreating as he laid her on the bed.

Her pulse sped up again though as he unbuttoned his shirt, then stripped it off.

Moonlight flickered over the tanned skin, putting the bunched muscles of his torso into stark relief. He was magnificent. Tall, muscular, lean and powerful. The dark hair that defined flat brown nipples and arrowed down into his trousers through his abs had her lungs seizing. Her throat dried as he released the hook on his suit trousers and kicked off his shoes.

The rigid erection sprang up as he lowered his boxers.

Her gaze met his, her breathing so shallow now it was a miracle she didn't faint as he climbed onto the bed.

'Lose the pants, *ma belle*,' he said.

She wriggled out of the sweatpants and flung them away. He climbed on top of her. His skin felt hot and firm as he pressed her into the mattress and a rough palm coasted up her bare thigh. A hoarse cry escaped her throat.

Their skin touched everywhere. His fingertips electrified her nerve endings as they found the sensitive seam of skin at the top of her thigh, then located the slick heat at her core.

'So wet for me, *ma belle*.' She could hear the hunger in his voice. 'Tell me what you like.'

I don't know.

She trapped the answer in her throat. And flattened her palms against the ridged muscles, stalling for time. She didn't know how to answer that question; no man had ever seen her naked before, let alone touched her, stroked her.

His thumb found the bundle of nerves again and she moaned, jerking her hips towards the intimate torture.

'You like that?' he asked as his thumb circled, not quite touching her again where she needed.

'Yes, yes, please do it again.' She didn't care any more about the naked need in her voice, the raw desperation. She wanted to feel that glorious release once more.

'Can I touch you, too?' she asked.

The deep groan against her neck felt like a benediction. *'Oui.'*

She slid her hand down his chest, feeling the muscles quiver. His whole body shook as she wrapped her fingers around the stiff column of flesh. She had a moment of panic as she gauged his size, his girth and the steely strength beneath the velvet-soft skin. How would anything that large and hard ever fit inside her?

But then his thumb found that devastating

spot between her thighs and every thought flew out of her head.

She stroked him as he stroked her. But where his caresses were firm and assured, her movements were jerky and uncertain. Still she took pleasure in his shudder when her thumb found the bead of moisture at the head of his erection. She could feel his passion building as the coil at her core twisted and tightened. Her knees fell open, her hips angling forward, in a wanton display of need she couldn't control. Her fingers gripped his rigid flesh as one blunt finger entered her, sinking into the tight flesh, his thumb still working her into a frenzy.

'You are very tight. It has been a while, yes?' he asked.

She nodded. Because what else could she say? It was a lifetime since she'd felt this good.

He swore softly in French, his hips driving into her hand, the hard flesh getting longer, thicker.

'Come for me again, *ma chérie*,' he demanded, and just like that the wave slammed into her, flinging her over that final peak.

She let out a hoarse moan as she fell to earth, sinking into the glorious oblivion. But as the afterglow settled over her like a glittering cloud, her fingers flexed on the erection. He was still rigid, still huge.

Leaning over her, he fumbled in the bedside drawer, the rip of foil was loud enough to be heard over her staggered breathing.

Lifting her hand from his erection, he kissed the knuckles. 'I cannot wait any longer,' he murmured, the urgency sending new ripples of longing through her exhausted flesh.

He rolled on the condom, then grasped her hips.

She felt the head of his erection probe, before he thrust deep.

Rending pain seared through her and she choked off a sob.

'Merde!' He reared back.

She bit into her lip to stop the cry of pain. Intense pleasure had turned to shock and discomfort, but far worse than the soreness where his erection was lodged deep inside her was the look of pure horror that shadowed Dominic's face.

He knew.

The thought doused the heat, until all that was left was the chill of his disapproval.

Of course, he knew. Why had she thought he wouldn't notice? A man with his experience, who had probably slept with dozens of women.

She shifted, trying to adjust to the thick length inside her, hoping to regain the desire that had disappeared in a rush. But his fingers flexed on her hips, and he flinched.

'Don't move,' he groaned. 'I don't want to hurt you more.'

'It's okay, it doesn't hurt.'

'Don't lie,' he said, his gaze shadowed now, the horror replaced with surprise and something that looked like guilt. 'I am your first. Is this not the case?'

She wanted to lie, to take the guilt out of his expression. But how could she, when it was clearly obvious?

'Yes, but it's not a big deal,' she murmured, because it really wasn't. Or at least it shouldn't have been. Up until the moment he had entered her, she'd been delirious with pleasure. He'd brought her to orgasm. Twice. And more than anything she wanted to do the same for him. To see him shatter the way he had made her shatter.

'I must withdraw,' he said.

'No, don't.' She clasped his shoulders. 'Don't stop. I don't want you to stop.' The tearing pain had already lessened, the tendrils of heat building again at her core, the pulsing ache becoming sharp and insistent.

'Damn it, Alison, you don't know what you ask of me. I am not sure I can be gentle.'

The growled admission, grudging and yet gruff with desperation, had her heart contracting.

'I don't need you to be gentle, Dominic. I just need you to treat me like a woman.'

To treat me like your *woman.*

The foolishly romantic thought echoed in her head.

She buried it deep. She hadn't lied when she'd told him her virginity was not a big deal to her. She was twenty-five years old. It was ridiculous she'd waited this long. And yes, it had hurt. But already the full stretched feeling had changed into something closer to pleasure than pain. He filled her up in a way that made her breath hitch, and her clitoris throb with renewed yearning.

'I'm not fragile,' she added, because he was still braced above her, not moving, his face strained with the effort it was taking him to hold still. 'Really I'm not. I know what I want.' *And what I want is you.*

She threaded her fingers into his hair, coaxing him to do what they both needed. He swore softly, but then placed a hand at her cheek, brushing his thumb across her lips.

'D'accord, ma belle,' he murmured, his gaze becoming dark and intense as he glided out of her, then thrust back in, slowly, carefully, sinking in to the hilt.

The head of his penis massaged a spot deep inside her and she gasped, the delicious shudder adding to the heat at her core.

'C'est bien?' he asked, his perfect English having deserted him.

'Yes,' she moaned. 'It's good.'

He established a rhythm—slow at first, and then building—digging at that spot ruthlessly, relentlessly as heat fired over her skin.

The waves of pleasure gathered again with each new thrust of his hips, each new jolt of desire. She clung to him, the only solid object in the storm engulfing her. Every pulse and heartbeat became attuned to the ravages of pleasure he was waging on her body. The steady rhythm became harder, faster, over-whelming, unstoppable.

She couldn't think any more, couldn't make sense of the sounds and sights around her, all she could do was feel…

Her moans became pants, her sex contracting, massaging the hard length. The brutal pleasure coiled tighter at her core. The edge of desire so sharp she felt buffeted, burned, undone.

Then his thumb found the swollen folds where their bodies joined, triggering a conflagration so fierce and all-consuming she cried out.

Her body arched into his, the shattering orgasm exploding along her nerve-endings, like a shimmering light, splintering and then retreating to splinter again.

She could hear her own sobs, her fingers fisting in his hair, as he finally let her tumble to earth—his shout of fulfilment following her over that high wide edge.

His big body collapsed on top of her, his raw pants matched hers, the musty scent of sex and sweat mingling with the shiver of surrender.

She hugged him, exhausted, spent. Her sex sore, her body limp. She caressed the silky strands at his nape now damp with sweat, and tried not to acknowledge the debilitating wave of emotion threatening to engulf her.

It's just sex. Just for one night. It doesn't mean anything.

But still she couldn't quite ignore the faltering beat of her heart at the realisation that, after twelve years, all her foolish teenage fantasises had finally come true. And it had definitely been worth the wait.

CHAPTER FOUR

BREATHE, DAMN IT. Breathe.

Dominic's hands slipped from Alison's hips as he withdrew. She flinched and the dart of shame stabbed at his chest.

His fingers shook as he imagined the bruising imprint of his thumbs on the soft skin where he'd gripped her as he'd pumped into her.

What the hell had just happened? Because what should have been a smooth, subtle seduction had become something frenzied and frantic.

He'd planned to make love to her tonight as soon as they had been alone together in the study—and he'd seen the arousal in her eyes.

She was beautiful, captivating, she wanted him. And she could solve all his problems.

Figuring out where his housekeeper had hidden the first-aid box downstairs had given him more than enough time to consider the tempting possibilities Alison Jones's reappearance in his life tonight might mean.

He needed a wife and she could be perfect for the role.

Not only did she turn him on to the point of madness, something Mira had never done, but he could offer her a home, and financial security. The fact she was completely unknown to the press with no scandal attached to her was another huge point in her favour. It would be a relatively simple job to set up a new PR narrative to explain their whirlwind romance and wedding. Mira had been out of the country for over a month, he and Alison had known each other as children, they'd met again when she'd delivered something to his home and one thing had led to another.

The only question had been whether she desired him, too. Had he imagined that spark? Because it suited his own ends so perfectly?

But as soon as he'd walked into the study and seen her face flush and her breathing accelerate, he'd known he hadn't imagined anything. And when he had touched her bare foot, and she'd nearly jumped out of the chair, he'd had to swallow a harsh laugh.

Game on.

But why hadn't he questioned her artless responses, the beguiling blush that had spread across her collarbone as soon as he'd started flirting with her?

She'd been as eager as him, that was why. He'd assumed the blush, the innocence were all an accomplished act, an act to disguise the fact she was more than ready to take Mira's place—especially when she had questioned him about the business deal.

He'd been in her situation himself, years ago when he'd been destitute after arriving in Paris with three broken ribs and not a penny to his name, so why would he judge her for taking the easy option? Of snagging a rich man? Hadn't his own mother—and hers—tried to do the same?

But once he'd tasted her, the sophisticated seduction he'd planned had changed into something elemental.

She had tasted like she smelled. Strawberries and chocolate. Sweet and decadent. But more than that, she had tasted of summer, and sunshine, and joy and surrender.

The fanciful thoughts had scattered, becoming dark and earthy and driven as she'd squirmed against his hardening erection, like a cat desperate to be stroked.

Bon Dieu, but he hadn't been able to get enough of her, exploring the recesses of her mouth like a man possessed.

And once he'd freed her breasts, felt her nipples harden and swell against his tongue, he'd been lost in a passion so intense it had been a major battle not to take her right there against the wall of his study.

When his hands had cupped her naked bottom, sensation had hurtled beneath his belt with the speed and accuracy of a heat-seeking missile.

Suddenly, he'd become the desperate boy again, instead of the experienced lover.

He'd had to force himself to slow down, to carry her to the bedroom and strip off his clothes, to draw forth another orgasm—simply to prove he could wait to have her, that he was still the one in control—before he'd plunged into her.

But when she had gasped and stiffened in pain, he'd known instantly—this was no act.

She had been a virgin, for God's sake.

He should have stopped then, but, even while he was frantically trying to assess the repercussions of her innocence, his body had refused to obey him once she'd given him permission to continue—so he'd taken what she'd offered, because he'd been unable to do otherwise.

And now here he was, lying in bed beside her, not knowing what the hell to say to her.

Should he apologise? Explain? She'd said it wasn't a big deal, but somehow it was to him. He'd never been a woman's first lover. Had deliberately avoided that sort of intimacy. And what did he do now about his plan to suggest they marry? Because this could complicate things in ways he did not want, and had not anticipated.

His gut twisted as he felt her shift on the bed beside him. She hadn't spoken, probably because she was as shocked by the intensity of their lovemaking as he was. And appalled by his lack of sophistication.

Or was she? How would she know the power of their connection—or how catastrophically he had lost control—if she had never slept with another man?

She sat up with her back to him, but as she

went to stand he flung his arm out and caught her hip. 'Where are you going?' he asked, pleased when the words came out reasonably smoothly despite the rawness in his throat.

She glanced over her shoulder. 'I hope you don't mind if I borrow your sweats? I'll return them tomorrow.'

What?

It took a moment for him to register what she was asking him and why as she bent down to scoop the sweatpants off the floor. But when she tried to stand, he at least had the presence of mind to keep his hand anchored on her hip.

'You're not going anywhere tonight, Allycat,' he said, moving across the bed to band an arm around her waist.

She twisted round again, her face so close he could see the confusion in her eyes. 'Why... why not?' she asked.

Mon Dieu, she was even more innocent than he had assumed.

He kissed her shoulder blade. 'Because I have exhausted you. And it is still raining.' They weren't the main reasons, not even close, but he didn't want to talk about anything else until he had calmed down enough to figure out all the angles.

Perhaps her virginity didn't have to be a bad thing. At least it seemed unlikely that as his wife she would be photographed kissing other men. And perhaps his spectacular loss of control was a one-off. She'd unsettled him the minute she had arrived. They had a history; she knew more about his background than any of the other women he had slept with. And he hadn't been with a woman in six weeks. Maybe he'd had longer dry spells before while he was building his business, but perhaps this need, this desperation, the intensity of their connection were nothing more than chemistry and opportunity.

'I thought I'd just get a cab, like you suggested,' she said.

Why had he suggested the damn cab?

'Alison.' He pulled himself up on the bed, and sat behind her, his legs straddling hers. He wrapped his arms around her waist, and dropped his chin on her shoulder. 'There is no need to leave. I want you to stay.'

The heat surged back into his groin—making the erection swell against her bottom.

She stiffened slightly. 'I don't… I'm a bit sore, I don't think I want to do it again tonight,' she said. And he was caught between a laugh and a groan.

'Ignore that, I have no control over my body's reaction to you.' Wasn't that the truth? 'I have no intention of touching you again tonight,' he said. He lifted the sweatpants out of her hands and then manoeuvred himself off the bed so he could stand and put them on. Grabbing the bathrobe that hung on the back of the bedroom door, he passed it to her.

She scrambled into it. He couldn't make out her expression in the half-light, but he could sense her embarrassment and uncertainty. And suddenly the pulse of reaction in his crotch wasn't nearly as disturbing as the pulse of something around his heart.

She was sweet and adorable and genuine, not something he usually looked for in a hook-up. But then she wasn't a hook-up; he was hoping she would agree to become much more than that, tomorrow. And for what he had in mind, perhaps her innocence could be a huge advantage.

But until he'd had a chance to consider his

plan carefully in light of this new information, he didn't intend to let her out of his house.

For tonight, though, it would be best if he kept her out of his bed. Or he would find it very hard to keep his promise—not to touch her again.

'Are you hungry?' he asked.

She shook her head. 'Just tired.'

'Then come with me,' he said, ignoring the renewed pulse of emotion as she hesitated before taking his hand.

He guided her out of the bedroom and into the study.

'There is another bedroom with an en suite on this floor.' He led her down the darkened hallway and across the landing to open the door to another of the house's six bedrooms. He leant against the doorframe as she stepped into the room.

'Get some sleep. I will see you in the morning.' Once he'd worked out exactly how to proceed.

She stood in the room, looking a little lost. 'But I left my bike outside,' she said.

He huffed out a strained laugh. 'I'll bring it in out of the cold.'

'Okay, thanks,' she murmured. 'For everything.' Then flushed, obviously realising the double meaning.

He had to hold back another harsh laugh.

Damn, but she really was utterly adorable. He grasped the lapels of her robe and tugged her close, but restricted the goodnight kiss to a chaste peck on her forehead. *'Bonne nuit*, Allycat.'

Tomorrow they would talk. But for tonight he needed space and distance; they both did. Their spectacular chemistry did not have to be a bad thing, in fact it could be a very fortuitous thing, and not just for his business.

But first he needed to ensure her innocence hadn't created complications he couldn't control.

CHAPTER FIVE

IT TOOK ALLY a moment to adjust to the dawn light shining through the open shutters of the big bay window when she woke the next day. She pushed herself up on her elbows, the sheet sliding over sensitive skin. It took her a moment more to figure out where she was.

Then the memories came flooding back in a dizzying kaleidoscope of scents and sights and sounds and sensations.

The crackle of the dispatcher's voice shouting out Dominic's name through the rain, the aroma of pine soap and whisky, the rich fruity taste of the Merlot, the flicker of moonlight caressing the muscular planes of Dominic's chest, the rending pain and then the shocking pleasure as he filled her to bursting.

And the confusing thoughts as she'd drifted into sleep afterwards.

She swung her feet to the floor and wrapped the sheet around her naked body, aware of all the places Dominic had caressed with such skill and efficiency the night before. Her breasts, her lips, her sex.

What she'd experienced had been so much more than she had been prepared for. She hadn't expected that level of pleasure, or that level of intimacy. How had he known exactly how and where to touch her? Was this what her mother had always craved, that pure physical connection? Was that why she'd exposed herself so easily? To so many men? After Pierre had discarded her?

A chill rippled over Ally's skin, even though the house's heating was set at the perfect ambient temperature.

Another thought intruded, of how Dominic had kept his composure last night, and she'd lost all of hers.

She walked across the room on unsteady legs and shrugged on the bathrobe he'd given her the night before, inhaling the scent of him, which still clung to the material. Then felt foolish.

She needed to leave. She should have left last night. Seeing him this morning would be awkward and uncomfortable for both of them—the fact of her virginity, and the lies she'd told to conceal it from him, not just an elephant in the room but a ten-ton pachyderm.

It was still early, she thought, assessing the light through the window. Probably only six, if that. She had time to take a quick shower, then hunt up her clothing, find her bike and get out.

But when she dashed into the bathroom, she spotted her reflection in the mirrored wall opposite the shower cubicle.

The sight stole her breath. She hadn't expected to look different, to feel different, had assumed that was a myth women told each other to make their first time have meaning.

But she did look different. Her hair was rumpled, her skin pink in places where his stubble had rubbed against it.

The stupid wave of emotion took her unawares.

Not a big deal. Not a big deal. Don't make too much of it.

A heavy weight sank into the pit of her stomach.

Don't you dare cry.

After a quick shower, she ran her fingers through her hair and stared at herself in the bathroom mirror, pressing her thumb against the skin of her cheek—tender from beard burn.

Last night had been an experience, an experience she refused to regret. But it was a new day now, the harsh light of the March dawn after the storm signalling a return to real life.

Tiptoeing down the hall, she slipped into the study, cold now with the fire burnt out. She found her bra on the floor where Dominic had discarded it.

Now all she needed was the wet cycling gear she'd left in the bedroom where they had made love. The door was ajar. She huffed out a shaky breath when she peered into the room to discover it empty, the large bed still rumpled from the night before.

A vision of Dominic's magnificent chest limed by moonlight blasted into her brain. The heavy sensation at her core throbbed.

She shook her head, trying to expel the dazed feeling.

So, so *not the point.*

She found her cycling gear where she'd left it, hanging over the heated towel rail in the bathroom. Dropping the robe, she slipped on the now dry clothing, easing the torn cycling pants over the bandage on her leg.

The memory of his fingers, gentle and efficient as he bandaged her calf, had the heat eddying back through her body. And the emotion squeezing her ribs. She breathed. In, out. And waited for the wave to pass.

But as she left the bathroom, she stumbled to a stop as her gaze connected with the unmade bed—and the pulse of guilt and yearning wrapped around her heart like a vice, the bloodstains on the bedsheet like a banner ad to her naiveté.

Had she really believed she could sleep with Dominic, have him be her first lover and suffer no emotional fallout whatsoever?

But even as she acknowledged the foolishness of that assessment, she refused to regret her decision. How many women could say they had been initiated into sex by their childhood crush—and got three amazing orgasms into the bargain?

Dominic and last night had been a gift. A gift she had deserved after the harsh realities of her life ever since that summer in Provence. Through the many dark days spent watching her mother become addicted to prescription painkillers, and throw herself at men who didn't treat her with respect, or kindness. Seeing her become a shadow of the beautiful woman she'd been that summer when Pierre LeGrand had loved her.

Perhaps it was ironic it was Pierre's son who had given Ally this boon, but why did it have to be significant?

She already knew the gift of great sex wasn't something that could last.

It was the one thing she had discovered while watching her mother sink into despair. That it was far too easy to mistake sex for love—and love, even when it was genuine, was totally unreliable.

It required you to allow your life, your happiness, to be dependent on the whims of others. She'd learned a valuable lesson in the last twelve years: not just that love could destroy you if you let it, but that survival meant relying on yourself and no one else.

The yearning she felt, the sadness that last night was never going to be repeated, was purely physical.

Dominic was a handsome, powerful and overwhelming man—and an experienced lover. And they had a past dating back to the days when she'd still believed in love and romance. Of course she'd been captivated by him.

But she could not allow what had happened last night to have any lasting significance in her life.

Plus she was never going to see him again—if she got a move on.

Once she was back on her bike, delivering pizzas and urgent documents and maybe even someone else's wedding ring—last night would all be a wonderful dream, which she'd be able to pull out of her subconscious and enjoy whenever she needed a pick-me-up or an incentive to get through another day.

She flung the sheets over the bloodstains, and sat down to wrestle her still-damp cycling shoes back on. Then walked back out of the room.

There was no sound coming from the floor below.

Thank God, she hadn't sabotaged her getaway with loads of pointless soul-searching.

She rushed down the wide sweeping staircase, then headed along the hallway towards the back of the house, retracing the steps she'd taken the night before; the cleats of her cycle shoes clattered on the polished wood flooring. She spotted her bike, parked inside the back door, and felt the tight feeling in her chest release—and her lungs deflate a little.

It's all good. A quick getaway is for the best, to save the discomfort of the morning after.

A rueful smile tugged at her lips. Never having had sex before, she didn't know the etiquette for a one-night stand, but even *she* knew the morning after was something best avoided. Especially if you'd effectively tricked your lover into taking your virginity.

But as she stepped past the door to the kitchen, a wry voice rang out.

'Alison, you're awake. I hope you slept well?'

Crap! She was totally busted.

Dominic sat on one of the stools next to a large breakfast bar. The doorway she was now standing in like a dummy led into a huge open-plan kitchen—its state-of-the art appliances and stark metal and glass design in striking contrast to the Georgian majesty of the rest of the house.

But it wasn't the kitchen design that had all her attention.

Her lover looked every inch the master of industry in a sharp two-piece business suit, polished loafers and a starched white shirt. Gold cufflinks peeked out from the sleeves of his jacket and she could spot a dimple in his chin she hadn't noticed the night before thanks to his now clean-shaven jaw.

Apart from the fluorescent lighting shining on his slicked-back hair, which suggested he'd showered fairly recently, too—probably while she was wasting time with all her pointless soul-searching over a couple of bloodstains—he couldn't have looked any more indomitable.

Her lover.

The words reverberated in her chest. Novel and delicious—and also ludicrous. Dominic wasn't her lover. He was a man she'd had one glorious night with.

As usual it was impossible to read his expression. The tenderness from the night before, when he had kissed her goodnight, was gone, replaced by a sensuous but oddly impersonal smile. He'd been in control last night, but he was even more so now.

She wrapped her arms around her waist, feeling naked beneath that searing gaze, despite her muddy cycling gear.

'How are you?' he enquired, his gruff French accent rumbling through the already far too sensitive parts of Ally's anatomy.

'I'm good, thank you,' her reply came out on an unconvincing croak.

Fabulous, Ally—can this actually get any more awkward?

She forced herself to release her arms and jerk a thumb over her shoulder. 'I was just heading off.'

'So I saw,' he said, the wry amusement not helping with her breathing difficulties. He beckoned her towards him. 'Come here. We need to talk.'

Her breathing accelerated.

What about?

She walked into the kitchen, her cleats clinking against the room's expensive slate flooring, her heartbeat gagging her.

He patted the stool next to him. 'Sit down.'

She did as she was told, aware of his gaze gliding over her bandaged leg. The rush of

adrenaline, the shot of heat melting her panties, only made her more self-conscious.

'How's the leg?' he asked.

'Great. Listen, I really don't have time to—'

'I have a proposition for you,' he interrupted
her, then placed his palm on a sheaf of papers
on the breakfast bar next to his mug of coffee,
and slid them towards her. 'It should be more
than worth your time to hear me out.'

'A proposition?' She glanced at the papers,
confused. They looked like legal documents.
Was he going to sue her or something? What
for?

'Yes, a proposition.' He tucked a knuckle
under her chin and forced her gaze back to
his. 'Don't look so scared, Allycat. This isn't
bad, it's good.'

The amused, assured tone hadn't faltered.

'What's the proposition?' she asked.

'You haven't guessed it already?' he asked,
and alongside the amusement she could hear
the cynicism, which had made her sad for him
the night before. It wasn't making her sad for
him now, it was making her sad for herself.
Had she ever been more clueless and out of
her depth?

'No,' she said, because she had no idea what he was talking about and there wasn't much point in trying to disguise it, however much she wished she could.

'I need a wife. And you would be perfect.'

'A…what?' she said, her mouth going slack with shock. But the way her heart was pinging around her chest cavity like a ball trapped in a pinball machine told a different story. 'Did you say a *wife*?'

Because she couldn't possibly have heard *that* right.

'Yes, as I told you yesterday. I have an important deal in Brooklyn that's about to go up in smoke if I don't find a way to persuade the conservative consortium who own the land that my private life is…' he shrugged '…stable. And not about to attract any unwanted scandal. I proposed to Mira to solve the problem, but marriage to someone like her would have created other problems. Trying to persuade anyone I was madly in love with her when I could hardly stand the sight of her would have required a level of acting talent I simply do not possess. You, on the other hand…' His gaze darkened as it drifted over her. The tug of desire became a sharp yank in the hot sweet spot between her thighs.

'I... I don't know what to say,' she said, because she really didn't.

She was still processing her shock. In truth, she ought to be horrified. He was proposing marriage as if it were a business transaction.

She wasn't a romantic, and she'd known he was a deeply cynical man, from the way he'd spoken about his broken engagement with Mira yesterday... And maybe even before that, all those years ago, when he'd seemed so much older than his sixteen years.

But if she was so shocked and horrified by the ruthlessness of his proposal, how exactly did she account for her pinballing heartbeat?

'I guess I'd need more details,' she said, to buy time, until her ricocheting heartbeat wasn't threatening to ping right out of her chest.

'Smart girl,' he said, his gaze still dark with desire, but his tone stark with pragmatism. 'I'd need you to sign a non-disclosure agreement and a pre-nup, on the understanding the marriage will only last as long as I need it to. And then we would divorce. It shouldn't tie up your private life for more than three or four months, six at the most. And I'm willing to offer you a generous settlement if you help me.'

'I don't want your money,' she said, her pride kicking in at last.

'Why not?' he said. 'When you can clearly use it.'

'Because it would make me feel compromised,' she said, finally finding the horror she'd been looking for.

Hadn't his father bought her mother for that one summer? Monica Jones had been Pierre LeGrand's mistress. Maybe Ally would never be gullible enough to misconstrue such an arrangement for love, but she wasn't about to offer herself for sale either. Not after she'd seen what it had done to her mother.

'How would you be compromised?' he asked, sounding genuinely confused.

'Well, because we'd be sleeping together, wouldn't we?' she asked.

He chuckled, and lifted his hand to run his thumb down the side of her face. The flare of desire in his dark chocolate gaze was intense and searing. 'I certainly hope so. Yes.'

She captured his finger, and dragged it away

from her face, resisting the urge to give into the fierce rush of need dampening her panties.

'Then, that's why,' she said, not sure where the prickle of disappointment was coming from. 'I refuse to become any man's mistress, the way my mother was. Your father bought and paid for her that summer. I know it was her fault she allowed herself to believe he felt more for her than he did, and that's why it broke her when he kicked us both out. I'd never make a mistake like that. But I still don't want to put myself in that position. With you or anyone else. It's demeaning.'

Dominic stared at the flushed and wary expression of the woman in front of him, which only made her face—the soft skin of her jaw rouged in places by the ferocity of his kisses the night before—more beautiful.

And wanted to punch a wall.

How could he have screwed up this negotiation, so fundamentally? He was an expert in the art of the deal; he knew how to get exactly what he wanted when hashing out a contract.

But as soon as he'd got everything straight in his head last night, then put in a call to his legal team, his emotions had been more engaged in this process than he would have liked—which was probably why he had made so many fundamental errors.

He couldn't risk Alison walking away from this proposal. He was running out of time and she was the perfect candidate to be his wife. She was smart and sensible and a realist. She'd had to live in the real world, unlike Mira, and, as she'd just stated, despite her inexperience she was not a romantic. And he still wanted her, even dressed in the muddy torn clothing; he would have quite happily lifted her up onto the countertop and started up where they had left off last night. In fact, as soon as he'd spotted her making a beeline for the back door, he had briefly considered trying to seduce her into agreeing to this marriage. The only reason he hadn't was that he knew she had to still be recovering from last night's excesses and he couldn't guarantee he could be gentle with her now any more than he had been able to last night.

And then there was the fact of her virginity. The more he'd thought about that last night, the more it had come to seem like a massive benefit instead of a complication.

One of the biggest problems with marrying Mira had been the thought of how hard it was going to be to persuade anyone he was in love with her. Helping Ally discover the limits of her own pleasure, showing her how much she had been missing, was a project he could get behind one hundred and one per cent—making it a great deal easier to pretend he loved her. Passion was often confused for love, after all.

He'd never slept with a virgin before, because he didn't want the responsibility, but he had never considered what it might be like to initiate a woman as innately passionate and responsive as Ally.

She had no idea how much fun they could have together. Hell, fun was too tame a word for what they could do together. On the basis of what they had shared last night, fun didn't even begin to cover it.

But he couldn't seduce her again until he'd got her to accept this deal. And he could see that what had happened between his pig of a father and her sweet, gentle, hopelessly vulnerable mother was going to be a major stumbling block. He should have figured that out sooner.

Luckily, he was good at thinking on his feet.

'To be clear, Alison,' he said, 'I won't be paying you for the sex. And you're certainly under no obligation to sleep with me. My hope was that you would want to. Last night demonstrated we have a rare chemistry...' Being a virgin, she probably didn't realise that. 'I'd love to explore that in the months ahead, making this a business arrangement with considerable benefits for both of us. But if that makes you feel demeaned, I won't press the point.'

He smiled, determined to put her at ease if it killed him.

'I certainly wouldn't expect you to sleep with me against your will.' That much at least he could be very clear on. 'And the divorce settlement I'm offering...' he placed his palm on the sheaf of papers he'd had his legal team and his accountants up all night preparing '...which includes a generous allowance and all your other expenses during the marriage plus a one-off alimony payment of a million pounds sterling when we part, is compensation for your time and your agreement to act as my devoted wife.

But only in public. What we do in private is entirely up to you.'

'A m-million pounds!' she stuttered, her pale skin flushing a deep dark pink. 'Seriously?'

She looked so shell-shocked, he found his lips quirking, despite all the missteps he'd made.

He still had the upper hand in this negotiation. Of course he did. Alison was an innocent. She'd never had another lover, and from the peaks of her nipples thrusting provocatively through the soft cotton of her cycling shirt it was clear she was no more immune to him than he was to her. Plus she could definitely use the money.

'I want you to marry me, Alison,' he said, while she struggled to close her mouth again. 'It would be a mutually beneficial agreement. I travel quite a lot and if the Waterfront deal goes ahead…' which it would as soon as he had this woman on his arm, because her integrity and honesty were as visible and beguiling as those thrusting nipples '… I'll be living in Manhattan, mostly,' he added. 'While I assume you'd want to continue attending college here? So I wouldn't require too much of your time once we have established the narrative. I would just require you to be available for events my wife would be expected to attend with me.'

He'd thought it all through. This relationship would be run on his terms and his timetable. Them having mostly separate living arrangements made sense. He *would* need to spend the majority of his time in Manhattan once this deal got the green light. And she could continue attending college in London. He didn't want this marriage to impact her life too much as it would only complicate things when they parted. And, in the unlikely event he did get bored with her, he would be able to control the amount of time they spent together.

'The narrative?' she asked. 'What narrative?'

'The narrative of our relationship,' he said. 'It is best to stick as close to the truth as possible. My publicist will work out a press release—but it will be along the lines that we knew each other years ago, got reacquainted when you made a delivery here while Mira was in Klosters and I broke off my engagement with her once I realised I was in love with you.'

'Do you think the press will buy that?' she asked. 'You only broke up with her yesterday.'

'I don't really care if they do or not. The important thing is that the Jedah Consortium believes our marriage is real—which they will once they see us together, all loved up for a few key events a week from now in New York.'

If she agreed to his proposal.

He didn't like that *if.* He wanted this settled. Now.

But she hadn't said a word. She still looked dumbfounded. He forced himself to take a breath. And back off a little, before he spooked her altogether.

Unfortunately, he didn't have the luxury of time. He had a Eurostar to catch in two hours for a meeting in Paris this afternoon, then he was travelling to Rome tomorrow for several days—and from there he would fly to New York to finish the final negotiations on the Waterfront deal. By which time, if he wanted the negotiations to go smoothly, his marriage needed to be finalised.

He waited for her to say something, but she simply stared at him.

'Do you have any questions?' he prompted as he glanced at his watch, unable to hide his impatience.

She nodded, and the tension in his chest eased.

'Could I have time to think about it?'

He had to bite his lip to stop the husky, self-satisfied laugh from bursting out of his mouth. This negotiation was already in the bag. Of course it was; he didn't even know why he had been concerned about it. If the price was right, anyone could be bought. Even a woman as artless and forthright as Alison Jones.

He didn't think less of her for it. Money was important. Something he had learned at an early age—while he and his mother had struggled to survive in the slums of Saint Denis on the outskirts of Paris, on the tiny amount she'd been able to scratch together working two jobs—after having been refused child support from the wealthy man who had discarded her as soon as she'd fallen pregnant.

Alison and her mother had struggled in a similar way after that summer thanks to their association with his father, by the sound of it. He had no idea how bad it had become, but he didn't doubt she had to be fairly desperate to be risking her life each night as a cycle courier simply to pay her rent. Alison, unlike the spoilt debutantes and career women he had dated in the past, had to know what real poverty looked like; he was offering her a route out of that.

'Unfortunately, I need a verbal commitment from you this morning,' he said. 'As I have to catch a train to Paris in…' he checked his watch '…one hour and forty-eight minutes. You can take your time to read through the paperwork and negotiate any changes with my personal assistant, Selene, before you sign. If you want to renegotiate the alimony payment I can be flexi…'

'I don't want any *more* money,' she said, sounding horrified. 'Are you nuts?'

He barked out a laugh, unable to stop his amusement at the absolute horror on her face.

'I'm not a complete mercenary,' she added forcefully.

'Noted,' he said, thinking she didn't seem that mercenary to him at all. If she'd pressed he would easily have been persuaded to up the lump sum to two million pounds.

Getting the Waterfront deal was worth a great deal more than that to him.

The pulse of arousal struck him unawares. And he was forced to admit it wasn't just the thought of signing that deal that was driving his enthusiasm. She really did look good enough to eat—her eyes wide with confusion and uncertainty. The desire to capture her strawberry and chocolate taste on his tongue was all but overwhelming.

A week-long cooling-off period wouldn't be a bad thing at all. He needed to get a choke hold on his hunger before he made love to her again. Or things had the potential to get out of control, the way they had the first time. He wanted to show her he could savour her, that she was worth savouring.

'Come here, *ma belle.*' Before he could second-guess himself, he snagged her wrist and tugged her into the space between his knees.

Inhaling her scent—strawberries and sin— he unfurled her fingers, which had tightened into a fist. Lifting her palm to his mouth, he bit into the soft flesh beneath her thumb. Her shudder of reaction had the heat swelling in his groin. He lifted his gaze to hers, and smiled at the shocked arousal on her face.

'I want very much to make you my wife, Alison. And I'm willing to admit my reasons for suggesting it are not all about business—nor are they entirely honourable.' In fact, if the ache in his crotch was anything to go by, he wasn't sure any of them were at the moment. 'I think the months ahead will be beneficial to both of us, in a financial sense. You'd be doing me a big favour and I'm willing to pay handsomely for your time, it's as simple as that. But this marriage could also be very entertaining for both of us, on the evidence of last night.'

He dropped her hand, and got down off the breakfast stool. Capturing her shoulders, he pressed a kiss to her forehead, forcing himself not to press, not to push, not to take what he so desperately wanted. If she agreed to his proposition, there would be more than enough time to enjoy their chemistry to his heart's content in the months to come.

'You have twenty-four hours to read over the paperwork but I need your answer now,' he said. 'What do you say, Alison? Will you marry me?'

It was wrong. She knew that. Wrong to marry for convenience, for a business deal and definitely wrong to marry him for money. Whatever he said, whatever qualifications he put on what he was offering her, a part of her knew she was basically selling herself.

Maybe she wasn't selling her body; that much was true. She believed he wouldn't press her if she told him she didn't want a sexual relationship with him, but they both knew the chances of that were precisely zilch now she'd experienced how wonderful he could make her feel.

She also knew he was right about the comparison to his father and her mother's relationship. It wasn't the same thing at all; she could see that now. In fact, it was exactly the opposite—Dominic was offering her marriage and security with no pretence of love, while his father had offered her mother nothing *but* the pretence of love.

And that was the real temptation, she realised. The offer not of marriage, but of security. She didn't want his one-million-pound divorce settlement and she'd tell his PA as much when they ironed out the details of the contract. Whatever he said, she knew her time wasn't worth that much money; it was absurd. But the chance to live in this beautiful house, to have her expenses paid for the next few months, not to have to worry about the rent or the bills or her college fees. To be able to devote her time and energies exclusively to her studies, to designing the collection she wanted to design, maybe even get some of her designs seen while she was playing his devoted wife at the high-profile events he'd talked about. And to travel to places like New York and Paris, places she'd never seen but always wanted to see. That was another major temptation.

And then there was the fairy tale of being with him at those events. That was a powerful temptation too. Because he fascinated her. He always had. She wanted to find out how he'd become so successful, what had driven him, what drove him still.

And let's not forget the sex.

Six months of sex with Dominic LeGrand was not to be sniffed at. After waiting for twenty-five years to discover what all the fuss was about, last night she'd found out. Big time. She wanted to know more. To know everything. And she couldn't think of a better tutor than a man who could make her spontaneously combust simply by crooking his finger at her and directing her to 'come here' in that demanding tone of voice.

Was it really so wrong to say yes to all of that?

As long as she kept her wits about her, and remembered that this was a temporary arrangement, which had a hard and fast sell-by date.

He was offering her a chance to change her life. Why shouldn't she take it?

Didn't she deserve this chance? After everything she'd been through? And she could help him too, to get his business to the next level.

She wanted to do that. If for no other reason than to say thank you to that rebellious boy who had made her feel special and important, once upon a time.

The buzz of the doorbell made her jump, jerking her out of her thoughts, and the frantic reasoning as she tried to make a decision.

'That will be the car to take me to St Pancras International,' he said. 'I'm sorry to rush you, but I need your answer, Allycat?' The request sounded casual, indifferent even, but she could see the muscle in his jaw flexing and the hooded look in his eyes.

He wanted her to say yes as much as she

wanted to say it, she realised. Even though he was trying hard not to show it.

That tiny glimpse of the boy she'd once known, who guarded his emotions, his needs and desires with the same ferocity she had learned to guard hers, was enough to release the dam forming in her throat.

'Okay, I'm in. Let's get married.'

Relief crossed his face first, almost as if he'd actually been in doubt about her answer.

'Fantastique,' he murmured.

A wide smile spread across his far too handsome features. And it occurred to her it was probably the first genuine smile she'd ever seen on his face.

The inappropriate joy exploded in her chest.

This isn't a real marriage, Ally. It's a fake one. For goodness' sake, get a grip.

Tugging a pen out of his jacket pocket, he scribbled something down on the legal papers on the breakfast bar. 'This is Selene's number. She is my personal assistant. She can arrange to have your belongings moved into this house while I am away. I want you to resign immediately from your job as a courier.'

'Resign?' she asked dumbly.

The smile widened as he gripped her chin between his thumb and forefinger and pressed a kiss to her mouth. 'Yes, my little daredevil. I don't want my wife's life put at risk before I have a chance to consummate our marriage.'

My wife? Consummate? Goodness.

She didn't have a chance to process the information—or the heat flooding through her system as his kiss became carnal—before he had torn his mouth away again.

'Hold that thought,' he said. 'Selene will liaise with my legal team once you sign the pre-nup, and the publicist about a press release. We will be married as soon as you land in New York.' His gaze raked over her figure, making her even more aware of her grubby, torn cycling gear. 'Selene can also arrange someone to buy you the right clothes. As irresistible as I find your current attire, I'm afraid it's not going to work at the sort of events you will have to attend as my wife.'

She didn't need a stylist. She could design and make her own clothes—she wanted to be a fashion designer, after all. But before she could point any of that out, he pulled the jewellery box out of his trouser pocket and flipped it open, to reveal the exquisite ring she'd delivered the night before. Her breathing stopped.

The doorbell buzzed again.

'Arrêtes!' he shouted, loud enough to be heard by his driver, and make her jump.

'As I have no engagement ring I would like you to wear this, to seal our promise.'

She nodded.

Lifting her hand, he threaded the ring onto her finger. It felt heavy, but not as heavy as the weight in her chest when he stroked the knuckle and smiled.

'It fits? *Oui?*' He sounded excited. But not as excited as she suddenly felt.

Excited and a bit dazed if she was honest—because the whole situation felt completely surreal.

Her gaze fixed on his. 'Yes, thank you. It's exquisite,' she said.

The quick grin dazzled her.

'Not as exquisite as you, *ma belle*,' he murmured. The doorbell rang again and he swore softly. 'I will see you in New York in a week's time.' Grasping her trembling fingers, he lifted her hand to his lips and pressed a kiss into her palm. 'Until then *au revoir*, Madame LeGrand.'

A startled breath expelled from her lungs as she watched him stride out of the kitchen to the waiting car.

CHAPTER SIX

I'M GOING TO be married. To Dominic LeGrand.

Ally repeated the information in her head as she stared at the woven strands of platinum and gold that Dominic had slid on her ring finger a week ago. She was still finding it difficult to grasp the reality of her situation though, the events of the past seven days whirring through her head.

She glanced out of the private jet's window as it banked into a turn over Brooklyn, ready for its descent into JFK.

Unfortunately, the sight of a city she had always wanted to explore did nothing to slow down the fleet of butterflies in her belly. That would be the same fleet of butterflies that had been going nuts in her belly ever since she'd agreed to Dominic LeGrand's proposal.

The butterflies whose wings had only got bigger and more manic when she'd moved into his town house later on that first day, her meagre stack of belongings looking overwhelmed by the expensive surroundings. Not unlike their owner, she thought with a huff of breath.

She'd signed the marriage contract the next day after a negotiation with his efficient and ridiculously friendly and accommodating UK assistant, Selene Hartley—who had been more than willing to have the one-million-pound alimony payment cut from the settlement. Given that the first payment of the allowance Dominic had stipulated in the contract had wiped out all her outstanding debts and paid the rest of her college fees, she felt that was more than fair.

The week that followed had been spent getting used to her new surroundings—not easy when there were six bedrooms and an espresso machine that could dumbfound a NASA technician—and designing and making a wardrobe fit for a queen, or rather Dominic LeGrand's high-society wife, which was a lot more exclusive. With her college closed for the Easter break, she'd used the full seven days to work on her collection. She'd set up a workshop in one of the mansion's spare bedrooms with the help of Dominic's housekeeper, Charlotte, and, after sourcing some stunning materials from a series of exclusive fabric retailers with the rest of that first allowance payment, she'd spent most days and every evening sketching and pinning and sewing. Working on the designs had helped to ground her, in between the daunting tasks of attending a doctor's appointment to get a prescription for the pill and being ferried in a limousine to a series of exclusive beauty salons and spas arranged by Selene.

In the last seven days she'd been buffed and plucked and moisturised in places she hadn't even known existed.

The plane descended, dropping through the late afternoon sunshine, the green and gold Le-Grand Nationale logo glinting on its wing.

Her newly trimmed and painted fingernails grasped the padded leather of the seat in a death grip as her stomach plunged.

Instead of parking at the passenger terminals, the jet rumbled towards a private hangar at the end of the runway, not unlike the one she had been driven to—in a limousine, of course—that morning in Heathrow.

She ran her palms down the tailored jacket of the silk trouser suit she'd finished the night before as she tried to stay focussed on her ring and her new job.

Of being Dominic LeGrand's wife.

Because this was a job, a job she was being well paid for, and she needed to remember that.

But as she waited for the jet's crew to finish the landing procedure—the butterflies began having a fit.

What on earth was she doing here? In this rarefied world. For goodness' sake, she'd never been on a budget airline before now—let alone a private jet.

The butterflies dive-bombed into her belly as she examined her suit for the five billionth time. Had she made a major error designing and making her own wardrobe for this trip? She had her own unique style, one she'd developed and explored during her two years of fashion college, and had enjoyed turning into reality during the long hours spent working at her sewing machine in the last week to help calm her nerves. But what if the clothes she'd designed were all wrong? She might have her own style, but it was an urban, edgy, East London style. How would it be received in the kind of circles Dominic moved in—circles she knew nothing about? What would he do if he found out she'd pocketed the money he'd given her to buy an exclusive wardrobe and made her own clothes? Especially if her designs made him a laughing stock? Would he be angry with her? Furious? Could he sue? Had she already screwed up the biggest opportunity of her life?

The increasingly frantic thoughts clashed with the dive-bombing mutant butterflies in her belly.

'Madame LeGrand?' The hostess smiled down at her, using the name on the travel manifest.

'Yes?' Ally croaked.

'Are you ready to disembark?' the hostess asked in her heavily accented English, the beatific smile not faltering.

Not at all.

As panic closed her throat she forced her fingernails to release their grip on the seat.

'The immigration officials have checked your documents and Monsieur LeGrand waits for you,' the hostess added, sweeping her arm towards the door of the aircraft in a polite indication for Ally to get a move on.

Ally understood; the poor woman had been on her feet for seven hours.

'Right, sorry,' she said, unlocking the seat belt and standing.

She brushed her trembling palms down the sheer blue silk. And made her way to the front of the plane.

As she stepped out onto the outer stairs, she spotted Dominic standing at the bottom busy tapping out a message on his phone with both thumbs. A man with a briefcase stood beside him who had to be the marriage officiant Selene had told her would be there to issue their marriage licence as soon as she arrived. Apparently the marriage itself would be performed tomorrow, as the law in New York required a twenty-four hour wait after the licence was issued. But it wasn't the thought of the formalities that had the dive-bombing butterflies going up in flames.

Even with his head bent, Dominic looked more gorgeous and overwhelming than he had a week ago. She couldn't help noticing how the seams of his shirt stretched over his biceps as she made her way down the gangway on unsteady legs. How could he seem part savage, even in a business suit?

He's going to be your husband. Seriously?

Her heels clicked on the tarmac and Dominic stopped typing.

His dark chocolate gaze coasted over her figure, burning right through the silk. His eyes flared as his gaze finally met hers, and her ribs tightened around her lungs like a vice.

'*Bonjour*, Alison.' The husky accent rippled through her, setting off bursts of sensation— and making her far too aware of the hours spent tenderising her skin in the spas and salons he'd paid for over the last week.

Was that why every inch of her body felt as if it were about to burst into flames too, along with the dive-bombing butterflies?

'How was your flight?' he asked.

'Great,' she rasped as he approached, and she became aware again of exactly how tall he was.

He had to be at least six foot three.

Thank goodness she'd used some of the money he'd given her to purchase a range of high heels. She was hardly a small woman, having reached her full height of five foot seven at the age of fifteen, but he dwarfed her, just as he had when they were kids. She'd been considerably shorter as a thirteen-year-old. But had he been this tall as a teenager? He certainly hadn't been this broad. Maybe it was the way he'd filled out that made him so much more intimidating.

Stop staring at his muscles.

She forced herself not to step back, but she couldn't hide the shudder of reaction when he took her hand and brushed a kiss across the knuckles.

'You look exquisite,' he said, the approval heating his dark gaze almost as disconcerting as the sensation now shooting up her arm and reigniting those flaming mutant dive-bombing butterflies in her belly.

'Thank you,' she said, but the praise hadn't helped to mitigate her nerves one bit.

He introduced her to the man standing beside him. The balding young man who had been especially hired from the New York City Clerks' Office verified her identity. After they had signed the forms, he issued their licence and explained he would return to perform the ceremony at Dominic's apartment tomorrow, at which point the marriage certificate could be issued.

'*Bon,*' Dominic murmured, after the clerk had smiled and left. 'Only one more day and we can get all the paperwork out the way.'

Ally shivered, knowing that, whatever the officiant said, this marriage was already binding, at least for her, because she'd made a promise seven days ago. A promise she had no desire to renege on.

She felt suddenly naked beneath Dominic's gaze, and the truth was she almost was. What had possessed her to wear nothing but a bra under the jacket?

You idiot! Ruining the jacket's line is not going to matter if you pass out at his feet before you even get a chance to say I do.

Dominic's lips quirked—the way they had when he'd proposed a week ago, as if he were sharing a private joke with her.

'Why do you look so terrified, my darling almost wife?' His gruff accent lingered on the word 'wife'—both provocative and possessive. 'I promise not to seal our bargain until we are somewhere private.'

The laugh she managed to huff out past her

constricted lungs didn't sound as confident as she'd hoped.

'That's good,' she said, tugging her tingling fingers out of his grasp—the thought of him sealing the bargain they'd made a week ago sending a battalion of pheromones hurtling to every one of her erogenous zones along with those blasted butterflies. 'I wouldn't want to get arrested my first ten seconds on US soil.'

He laughed, the rough sound raw enough to stimulate her nerve-endings even more.

'*Touché*, Alison,' he murmured, the admiration in his dark hooded eyes so compelling she found herself basking in his approval. Even though she knew she shouldn't.

It's a job. It's a job. It's a job.

But the reminder couldn't stop the flaming mutant butterflies in her belly from going berserk as his warm arm banded around her waist and he led her across the tarmac to a waiting car—which was a huge black limousine. Of course.

Dominic clicked his seat belt into place, thankful for the physical restraint as the jacket Alison was wearing opened to reveal a seductive hint of purple lace while she strapped herself into the car next to him.

She looked absolutely exquisite, her willowy frame displayed to perfection in the striking blue suit, the shadow of cleavage making it hard for him to concentrate on anything other than the desire to get her back to his apartment as soon as physically possible.

He'd prepared for her arrival today by convincing himself his physical reaction to her a week ago had been exaggerated thanks to his long sexual drought, and the expediency of ensuring she agree to become his wife.

But as soon as he'd heard her heels on the tarmac, and looked up from his smartphone, he'd known he'd been kidding himself.

Dressed in grubby Lycra or oversized sweats, Alison Jones had been subtly sexy. Now she was stunning.

Long, slim, and stylish, her figure in the tailored suit looked both toned and athletic while at the same time being supremely feminine. And her striking bone structure, the translucent skin and those bottomless eyes the colour of a fine whisky, only enhanced by the hint of eyeliner and the lush sparkle of lip gloss, made her irresistible.

He wanted to undo the one button holding her jacket together, capture her full breasts in his palms and fasten his lips on the rampaging pulse fluttering in the delicate well of her collarbone.

The driving need to take her to bed as soon as was humanly possible was so strong, in fact, it had the potential to be problematic.

He didn't like being ruled by his desires—as much as he enjoyed sex, he had never had a problem controlling his hunger before now—and becoming addicted to Alison was not supposed to be part of this arrangement.

So stop leering at her and start talking.

He dragged his gaze away from her cleavage as the car left the airport and headed onto the expressway. She had her nose pressed against the window, obviously absorbing every new sight and sound, like a child outside a candy store.

'So you've never been to the States before?' he asked.

Her head swung round. 'I've never been anywhere before,' she said with an unabashed smile. 'Apart from Provence. But I've always wanted to come here. It's so exciting. Like being in a movie.' Her unguarded enthusiasm, like everything else about her, was utterly beguiling.

Her expression sobered suddenly, so much so he could see the nerves. He wondered what on earth she had to be nervous about.

'By the way, could I ask you something about the events we'll be attending while I'm here…?' she asked.

'What about them?'

'Do you think…?' She paused and bit into her lip, sending another shaft of heat straight to his groin.

'What is it?' he demanded, more curtly than he had intended as the lip bite tortured him. Was she doing it deliberately? If only she were, he thought, feeling less and less in control of the situation. But somehow he doubted it. Because… She had been a virgin.

What had seemed like such a boon before he'd married her—PR wise—seemed less so as the hot blood surged to his crotch with very little provocation. Why did the fact of her inexperience make him all the more eager to explore every aspect of her pleasure?

'I just wondered, do you think this outfit will be suitable?' she finally blurted out.

'Excusez-moi?' he asked, because it sounded as if she'd just asked him to give her fashion advice.

'This outfit?' She spread her arms wide, making the button strain even more.

He stifled a groan.

'Do you think it would work? For the kinds of events you were talking about...'

Mon Dieu, she *was* asking him for fashion advice.

'Selene gave me an itinerary,' she continued, the words pouring out as her nerves got the better of her. 'So I know what we're doing. But I've never been to the theatre before. Or the opening of an art gallery... So I had to wing it, and rely on some Internet research to figure out what to...' A guilty flush flowed into her cheeks. 'What to bring with me.'

He sat for a moment, trying to wrestle his libido under control and come up with a credible answer. Because it seemed to be important to her. And silently cursed his personal assistant. Why hadn't Selene employed an expert to help Alison with her wardrobe? Surely there were people who could advise you on your clothing? He was fairly sure he'd shelled out a small fortune for such a person for Mira. But it was too late to suggest that now. He didn't want to make her more nervous or unsure of herself.

'Alison, your outfit is stunning,' he said with feeling, giving the flowing lines of the suit another once-over. That at least was certainly not a lie. 'It will do perfectly.'

Who the hell cared if what she was wearing was the norm, or suitable? he decided. She looked incredible in the suit—enough to tie his libido into knots in sixty seconds or less.

'You really think so? You like the suit?' she asked, and he could hear her insecurity again. 'It's what you had in mind?'

'I *love* the suit. And I didn't have anything particular in mind,' he said, because the truth was what she would be wearing had not featured at all in any of the many, many erotic fantasies he'd entertained about her in the last week. 'Women's fashions are not my forte,' he added, just in case that wasn't entirely obvious.

'But on the basis of this outfit, I'm looking forward to seeing whatever else you've selected for this trip.' Which wasn't truth either, because he'd been looking forward to stripping her out of her new wardrobe a great deal more. But the tentative smile that curved her lips made him glad he'd lied. 'Does that set your mind at rest?' he finished, trying to keep his mind at least nominally out of his pants and on the main reason why she was with him in New York.

Good to know at least one of us is able to do that.

The sheen of pleasure made the amber of her eyes twinkle in the sinking sunlight streaming through the car window, the distinctive hue becoming all the more captivating.

His pulse bumped his own collarbone as the irony of the situation occurred to him.

How exactly had he ended up having to persuade his own fiancée how attractive he found her?

'I'm so glad you like it,' she said, emotion thickening her voice. 'It means a lot to me.'

He steeled himself against the visceral tug of

heat in his groin and the unsettling realisation she was genuinely moved by his compliment.

He'd never had a problem complimenting women on their appearance, especially when they looked as exquisite as Alison did in that moment, but there was something about her gratitude that reminded him of the little girl who had followed him around that summer, and how he'd clung to the open adoration in her eyes.

He cut off the thought, determined to forget the lost children they'd been that summer.

He wasn't that reckless, unhappy boy any more, desperate for any sign of approval. And she wasn't that little girl who had showered him with such unguarded affection.

He'd needed her to like him all those years ago—because under the veneer of teenage hostility and indifference, he'd been scared and confused, unable to understand why his father hated him so.

But he certainly did not need Alison—or anyone else—to like him now.

His phone vibrated, breaking the strange spell. He pulled it out of his pocket. And read the text from his business manager.

We have a problem with the Consortium. Mira Kensington just sold her story to the London Post.

He swore viciously under his breath and clicked on the call button.

Stop being a damn sap, LeGrand. Time to focus on what this marriage is actually supposed to achieve, instead of what it isn't.

'Dominic, is everything okay?' Ally asked as her fiancé swore in French.

'Yes, but I need to take this call,' he said, his tone curt and dismissive.

Everything didn't sound okay as he spoke in hushed tones to whoever was on the other end of the line in a stream of furious French.

After picking up that the conversation had something to do with Mira, she turned back to the window and tried not to listen.

Because thinking about his ex-fiancée would destroy the happy buzz his compliments had triggered.

A happy buzz that had gone some way to controlling her nerves—and all the feelings of inadequacy that had hijacked her during the flight.

Maybe it was pathetic how much she had enjoyed hearing him say he loved her outfit. And she probably ought to be shot for fishing for a compliment so shamelessly, but still his hot, unguarded approval had meant something.

She'd always believed that fanciful little girl had died after the summer in Provence. Because ever since that night she'd been forced to grow up, be a realist, not dream too big or too passionately, because she hadn't wanted to risk having her spirit crushed again. But that little girl hadn't died, she'd just been waiting for an opportunity like this.

Hearing Dominic's praise for her work, and knowing it was genuine, even if their marriage would be fake, had made her feel as if that child was able to believe in herself again... At least a little bit. And that felt liberating and empowering in a way she hadn't felt in a long time.

The car crossed the Brooklyn Bridge into Manhattan. The legendary skyline rose on the other side of the East River, the skyscrapers like silent sentries to the city's wealth and prominence.

As they drove through downtown she gazed in awe at the canyons of steel and glass and the bustle of traffic and people at street level—like London but so much more urgent, and manic, and less restrained. But as she heard Dominic finish his call it was hard for her to stay focussed on the excitement of being in a new city for the first time in her life.

His tension was palpable as he shoved his phone back into his pocket.

She had caught snippets of the conversation. Her French certainly wasn't fluent, but as well as Mira's name being mentioned several times she'd heard the word *'vierge'*.

Virgin.

Had Dominic been talking about her virginity to someone? Because she didn't even know how to feel about that. Embarrassed mostly, but also confused. Why would that be relevant, to anything at all? The only way to find out what was going on, though, was to ask.

The muscle in his cheek was flexing as he stared out of the window, obviously thinking something through.

'Is there a problem?' she asked.

His head turned. He looked as if he was angry, but trying not to show it.

'No,' he said, too dogmatically to be entirely believable. She might know nothing about his business, but she knew when she was being hoodwinked.

'If there's a problem, I might be able to help,' she said.

The hard line of his lips quirked in a reluctant smile. 'Are you serious?'

She nodded. 'Yes, I am.' She had no idea why he found that amusing, but she decided him being amused was better than him being furious. 'The only reason I'm here is to help you get this deal sorted out.' She coughed slightly, as the blush burned in her cheeks. Okay, that was a blatant lie. 'Well, the *main* reason I'm here is to help you get this deal sorted out.'

'Is that so?' he asked, his eyebrows launching up his forehead as he choked out a laugh.

'Well, yes,' she said.

'*Dieu*, Alison. Have I told you yet how damn adorable you are?'

'Maybe,' she said, glad to see him smile. But even gladder she'd caused that smile.

Especially when he picked up her hand,

opened her fingers and pressed his lips into her palm.

Her fingers curled around his cheek, heat shooting into her abdomen.

'Damn but I want you so much,' he said. The admission sounded a little tortured—which made her smile even more.

'Well, good,' she said. 'Because so do I.'

'Bien,' he murmured, with that hot possessive look in his gaze that was guaranteed to get the mutant butterflies partying in her pants.

He clasped her hand, and squeezed it. 'Okay, if I tell you what the call was about, will you promise not to be offended?'

'Of course,' she said. Confused now. Because he looked pained. And the slash of regret wasn't his usual default. He struck her as a man who made a point of regretting nothing.

'That was my business manager, Etienne Franco, on the phone. The consortium are questioning the validity of our love match because my former fiancée decided to give an exclusive interview to a British tabloid newspaper, which implied you're...' He paused, the muscle in his cheek flexing again. 'How did she put it in the article? "Being paid to service my sexual appetites while posing as my wife.'"

Ally cleared her throat, not sure what to say, because although she knew she *should* be offended by Mira's comments, the fact he seemed to be offended enough for both of them had a bubble of pleasure forming in her throat.

'That's a bit unfair,' she said, trying to sound stern while the bubble of pleasure burst, creating a warm glow through her entire body. 'Seeing as she's never even met me—well, not properly,' she corrected, remembering the altercation on the street.

Damn it, why isn't she furious?

'Alison, it's not just unfair of her. It's libellous. She's basically suggesting you're a prostitute in a national newspaper.' Dominic ground out the words, still so furious with Mira he could barely speak. But the truth was he was just as disgusted with himself. He should have guessed his ex would pull a stunt like this. And he hadn't done a damn thing to prevent it, or protect Alison.

In fact he'd basically set her up for exactly this kind of attack.

An attack that she was uniquely vulnerable to, not just because she appeared to have no sense of guile whatsoever, but because, as he had just discovered, she had been in much harsher financial straits than he had assumed.

As well as Mira's bitchy comments, the *Post* article had included a detailed description of the harsh realities of Alison's life before he had 'plucked her from obscurity'—and it had turned his stomach. The struggles she'd faced in the last twelve years had been a great deal harder than he had imagined. It seemed she and her mother had been living in abject poverty through her teens—ever since the night his father had thrown them off the estate. Alison had been supporting them both since the age of fifteen with a series of part-time jobs. And her debts had only increased after her mother's death from an overdose of prescription painkillers four years ago.

He'd exploited her destitution to feed the rags-to-riches Cinderella narrative his publicist had used to explain their 'fairy-tale romance' but now it had backfired on him spectacularly. Because he'd had no idea how close it was to the truth.

His father had destroyed her life that night… But his father hadn't been the only one responsible for what had happened to Monica and by extension her daughter.

He pushed the bitter memories to one side.

Do not go there. You can't go back and solve what you did.

But, unfortunately, telling himself that didn't make him feel any less responsible. Not just for what had happened that night, but for the trashing of Alison's reputation now.

'I'm going to sue her and the newspaper. I refuse to have you slandered in that way,' he said, because that at least was explainable.

Maybe his marriage to Alison was essentially a business arrangement, but by this time tomorrow she would finally be his wife, so of course he would have to protect her reputation.

'Wouldn't it be better just to ignore it?' Alison asked, her teeth tugging on her bottom lip again, and sending a now incendiary shot of heat to his groin.

'No, it would not.'

'But, Dominic, what about the Waterfront deal?' she said as his furious thoughts galloped ahead of him.

'What about it?' he barked. Why was she being so damn reasonable and accommodating about this outrage?

'Surely getting embroiled in a legal battle with a British tabloid isn't going to be good for that? Especially if they find out our marriage *is* essentially a business arrangement after all.'

I don't care about the damn deal.

He opened his mouth, to say the words that ricocheted through his consciousness. Then closed it again. As his fury and indignation slammed into a brick wall.

What the hell had he just thought? Hell, what had he almost said? Out loud?

He *did* care about the deal. The deal was everything. The deal was why Alison was here. Why *he* was here. The only reason this marriage was happening. And she was right: if he sued Mira and the *London Post* the real reason behind their marriage would come to light.

'The deal will be fine,' he said, even though he wasn't entirely sure.

Calm the hell down and think.

'I told the business manager to point out to the consortium you were a virgin. That you have never slept with another man before you slept with me. Making you the furthest thing from a prostitute.'

The foolish spurt of pride hit him unawares—the way it had when he had told Etienne.

What the heck was that about, too?

Alison's lack of experience was something he could use, to help make their marriage seem more authentic and to help him secure this deal. That was the only reason it was relevant. Why should he care if he was her first?

'Oh,' she said as a delectable blush rioted across her cheeks. And he almost laughed at the irony.

She was embarrassed about her virginity, but not about being dubbed a prostitute in a British tabloid.

'Did you *have* to tell him that?' she said. 'It's so personal.'

'I know, and I apologise, but I wanted to refute Mira's claims in the strongest possible terms.'

To secure this damn deal, which I completely forgot about a minute ago. Mon Dieu, *LeGrand, get a grip.*

'They're not going to put *that* in the papers, are they?' she asked, sounding horrified.

The rough chuckle burst out without warning. After all the fury and recriminations, the agony of knowing he'd failed her—and jeopardised the deal, which was of course much more important—her reaction seemed hopelessly naïve, but also ridiculously endearing. So endearing it managed to achieve several things at once—defuse his temper, restore his sense of humour and, most importantly of all, restore his sense of perspective.

He'd overreacted, not just to Mira's attack, but also to the disturbing news about Alison's circumstances in the last twelve years. That much was obvious.

What had happened on that night twelve years ago had no bearing on their circumstances now. And yes, maybe he was using Alison, but he had been upfront about that and she had made an informed decision to sign the contract. She was on board with all of this. And he was paying her a million pounds for her pains. He hadn't deceived her or seduced her into this situation. She had come of her own free will.

Alison was also correct. Ignoring Mira's attack made sense—the story would die a death more quickly that way. He'd already told Etienne about Alison's unsullied state to refute the claims made in the article with the consortium. And displaying their happy marriage for all to see over the next few days by escorting his new wife to a few high-profile events would hardly be a chore given that he was struggling to keep his hands off her.

The reason he had lost perspective about Mira's article and its fallout was even easier to explain.

An idiotic part of him had panicked that Alison might back out of their arrangement at the eleventh hour—thanks to the frustrating extra twenty-four hours the officiant had insisted they would have to wait before dotting the last of the *i*'s on their deal. Plus he'd waited seven whole days to consummate this damn deal already—while enduring the sort of sweaty erotic dreams every night that hadn't plagued him since he was a boy.

But Alison wasn't going to back out of this deal. And he didn't need to wait any longer to seal their deal, in the only way that mattered.

'No, they won't put it in the papers,' he said. But couldn't resist the urge to run a thumb over her lips. The sooner he fed this hunger, the sooner it would stop messing with his head. 'But why are you embarrassed about it?'

'Probably because I'm twenty-five years old and being a virgin at that age makes me seem sad and like a bit of a freak!'

'Firstly, you're not a virgin any more,' he said, unable to keep the smugness out of his voice. 'And secondly, I don't think it makes you a freak. It simply makes you discerning. You waited, until a man came along who was a good enough lover to give you the spectacular experience you deserved for your first time,' he added, teasing her now—and going the full smug in the process. 'Which isn't sad, it's smart.'

She huffed out a laugh, but the sparkle of amusement in her eyes was like a drug. When, exactly, had making her smile become so addictive?

'Spoken like a guy with an ego the size of Manhattan,' she said, but the embarrassed flush had begun to fade, so he considered her mockery well earned.

'*Touché*, again, Alison,' he said, grinning back at her as the car stopped in front of the loft apartment building he owned in Nolita.

Nolita, short for North of Little Italy, was the thriving neighbourhood that had been up-and-coming in the nineties but had now firmly arrived, with a young, trendy, arthouse crowd moving in to the turn-of-the-century brownstones and rehabbed tenement blocks.

'What a beautiful building—is this where you live?' Alison asked, her enthusiasm making his ribs feel suspiciously tight.

He'd bought the condemned brick and cast-iron building on the corner of Lafayette five years ago for a steal, then proceeded to work a miracle—gutting and then refurbishing the structure to preserve its historic integrity in the elegant arched windows and cast-iron balconies, while at the same time giving it a luxury, high-spec interior. The ten-storey block now housed the offices of LN's US-based operation, and a four-bed, four-bath penthouse loft apartment where he stayed when he was in the city.

'Yes, I own the building. LN's offices take up the first nine floors and then my apartment's on the top,' he said, then realised he was boasting and didn't know why. He'd never felt the need to impress a woman before.

'It's gorgeous,' she said. 'I love the art deco details.'

He got out of the car, not sure why his chest tightened even more at her praise. 'I'm glad you approve.'

He offered his hand and she took it.

The lapels of her suit jacket—the jacket that had been driving him wild as soon as she'd stepped onto American soil—spread as she stepped out of the car, giving him another provocative glimpse of pale flesh and purple lace.

The familiar shot of adrenaline pounded back into his crotch.

The chauffeur stepped to the back of the vehicle to help the doorman with their luggage, leaving them cocooned on the sidewalk, the car door shielding them from passers-by. He couldn't see any photographers, even though Etienne had suggested they might be besieged for the next few days as a result of Mira's story.

But he found himself tugging her into his arms regardless.

He'd waited seven days to get his mouth on Alison again. And now she was as good as his wife, what better way to finally put his idiotic overreaction to bed and get this agreement back where it was always supposed to be?

He placed his hands on her hips, until she stood flush against his body.

'Madame LeGrand,' he murmured. 'Time to start practising your act as the dutiful wife.'

Although it didn't feel like just an act any more.

But then, it wasn't an act, entirely. This was always supposed to be a business arrangement with benefits. So why not start claiming the benefits?

She looked up through long lashes, her amber eyes like those of a doe who had spotted the huntsman taking aim. And it occurred to him how inexperienced she still was. The punch of lust at the thought that she had only ever been his was visceral and basic and impossible to deny—so he didn't even try.

Her virginity had clearly turned him into a caveman. But he could do nothing but run with it now.

She lifted her arms and flattened her palms on his chest—the movement as brave as it was arousing.

'Es-tu prêtes?' he whispered against her neck,

his ability to speak English deserting him momentarily as he inhaled the rich, fresh scent of her, that glorious combination of strawberries and chocolate that had driven him wild in London—far too long ago.

Are you ready?

'Very,' she whispered back, her body shivering with reaction as he pressed his lips to the flutter of her pulse beneath her ear.

Plunging his fingers into her hair, he felt her soft sob against his lips before he angled her head and plundered. But as soon as his tongue tangled with hers, the surge of adrenaline became an unstoppable force.

He thrust deep, setting up an erotic rhythm spurred on by the grinding hunger beneath his belt.

She responded instinctively, her body surrendering to his will, her soft curves yielding to the hard contours as he pressed her back against the car's paintwork.

Had he ever been this desperate before, the need to rip off her clothes and plunge into the tight wet heart of her all but overwhelming? His hand slipped inside the open lapel of her jacket beneath the lacy bra until he was cupping the soft flesh of her breast, rejoicing in the feel of her nipple swelling against his palm.

'Mr LeGrand, do you have anything to say about Mira Kensington's piece in the London papers?'

The shouted question had him rearing back just as a camera flashed in his face.

Alison gasped and stiffened. The shocked arousal in her eyes turning the hot blood now running through his veins to wild fire.

The reporter stepped closer to shove a microphone between them as she scrambled to right her clothing.

The son of a...

'Get away from my fiancée,' he shouted in English, then repeated the command in French with a great deal more emphasis. The man seemed to get the message because he scurried away with his photographer.

Dominic grabbed Alison's hand.

'Let's finish this in private,' he said, realising the mistake of kissing her in public. He wanted to convince the consortium this relationship was real—but having a photograph of him baring her breast on the sidewalk emblazoned on the celebrity blogs would be counterproductive.

An older woman winked at him as he marched past. And a couple of teenage boys whistled from their spot on a nearby wall.

Dieu, *forget the paparazzi—he'd just put on a show for the whole damn neighbourhood.*

Leading Alison to the elevator at the back of the lobby, he stabbed the button. Damn it, he'd been about to take her right there on a public street.

He hadn't been aware of anything, not of the reporter or the photographer, who'd probably taken more than a few pictures, or the people watching, all he'd been aware of was her—the feel of her soft flesh cradling his erection, her fingers massaging his scalp, the drugging taste of her invading his nostrils and overwhelming his senses, the feel of her nipple hardening in his hand.

The elevator arrived quickly and whisked them to the top floor.

As they walked into the apartment her hand flexed in his and he heard her breath catch.

'Wow, what an incredible view,' she said.

He let go of her, and tried to focus. To give her a moment. To give them both a moment—

before he dragged her straight from the street into the bedroom.

Iron colonnades broke up the penthouse's vast open-plan living space. The designer had insisted on lots of rugs and some bespoke pieces of furniture to warm the harsh concrete floors. Several stories higher than the surrounding buildings, the penthouse's leaded glass walls afforded incredible one-hundred-and-eighty-degree views of the neighbourhoods of SoHo and Little Italy. The Empire State stood proud to the north and the new World Trade Center rose like a phoenix from the ashes of Ground Zero to the south.

The breathtaking view was the apartment's signature feature, but he couldn't even see it because all he could focus on was Alison as she spun round in a circle to capture it all, her cheeks reddened from his kisses. He rubbed his chin and encountered the beard scruff he hadn't shaved since that morning—he needed to slow the hell down. Give her some time to adjust.

But as his erection pounded in his pants, the way it had done every night he'd spent in his bed here alone, the only way he could think of to handle the hunger was to feed it.

'Alison, do you want a tour of the apartment or to finish what we just started on the street outside?' he managed.

Maybe his voice sounded rough and raw, and demanding, but he was giving her a choice, damn it.

She blushed deliciously, her gaze settling on the prodigious erection tenting his pants. 'I'm sorry,' she said.

'Don't be sorry.' He took her hand, squeezed it to reassure her. 'Just tell me you want this as much as me.'

'I do.'

It was all the permission he needed.

Tightening his grip, he led her across the living space towards the master bedroom.

As soon as they were inside, he slammed the door, and unhooked the button on her jacket that had been tormenting him since she'd stepped off the plane. He slid the jacket off her shoulders. The soft flesh of her breasts was pushed up like an offering in the purple lace. He slid his thumbs into the waistband of the suit's trousers, but couldn't seem to find the fastening.

'Take them off. I need you naked,' he demanded, deciding he couldn't waste time searching for it. His hands were starting to shake.

She quivered, and drew a zip down at the side of the trousers. He was glad to see her fingers were as shaky as his.

'Lose the bra, too,' he said, and watched as she freed her breasts from the lacy confinement.

But as he hooked his fingers in the elastic of her panties, ready to drag them off, she pressed a trembling hand to his shirt. 'Please, I need you naked too.'

The surge of desire at the urgency in her voice had his groin throbbing so hard he was scared he might explode too soon.

Don't be insane, you have never done that. Not even as an untried kid.

He shucked his own clothes in record time, then tumbled her onto the bed. The bed he'd dreamed about having her in far too often in the last week.

But instead of climbing up there with her—

and ending this even sooner—he grasped her hips, tugged her closer until she was sitting on the edge and knelt down, his knees sinking into the rug.

The sharp gasp as he hooked one of her legs over his shoulder, exposing her completely to him, only increased the surge of desire.

He pressed his face into her sex, inhaling her intoxicating scent. *Dieu*, but she smelt delicious—not just of strawberries and chocolate, but of heat and desire. He blew against the trimmed triangle of chestnut curls and licked the slick seam.

She moaned, her fingers plunging in his hair. He tasted her, circling, tantalising, listening to her throaty sobs, learning her contours, finding what she liked, and what she loved. Holding her open with his thumbs, he found the hard, swollen nub with his lips and suckled hard.

She cried out, jerking as the spontaneous orgasm ripped through her. His erection hardened to iron. Her juices soaked his tongue as he lapped up the last of her pleasure.

He rose over her.

With her skin flushed, her nipples begging for his attention, her body sated, and her eyes dazed, she was like a banquet laid out before him. The vague thought occurred to him that he might never get enough of her.

But then the need to feast on her overwhelmed him.

Ally's breath clogged, her sex already tender from Dominic's mouth as he notched the huge head of his erection at her core. And thrust deep.

The tight sheath stretched to receive him this time, the pleasure becoming so intense as he filled her, it was almost pain.

He rocked out, thrust back, ruthlessly stroking the spot he had found a week ago, working her into a frenzy of need. The orgasm exploded from her core this time, in shattering waves of sensation.

The desperate pants, the moaning sobs turned to hoarse cries of agony and then ecstasy as the wave crashed over her.

He grunted, and hot seed exploded inside her.

He groaned and collapsed on top of her.

She held him, her fingers shaking. Her body drifting in afterglow as her lungs seemed to collapse in her chest.

Why was she struggling to breathe? She'd climaxed. The sex was as good if not better than their first time.

He groaned and rolled off her, easing the still large erection out of her with some difficulty.

'I forgot to ask,' he said. 'Are you on the pill?'

The tightness in his voice made the breath thicken in her lungs.

'Yes.'

'Dieu merci,' he whispered, his relief palpable.

Thank God.

It was one of the stipulations in the contract she'd signed. He'd provided a detailed medical report to prove it would be safe for them to have unprotected sex, but had requested that if she agreed to a sexual relationship with him, she would also arrange oral contraception.

The clause had made sense to her at the time she'd signed it. Neither of them wanted an accident. Risking bringing a child into a situation like theirs would be disastrous—but as she lay beside him, the scent of sex and sweat surrounding them, his question had an odd shaft of melancholy rippling through her tired body.

Because it reinforced the limits of this relationship.

Not that she needed to have them reinforced.

She looked away from him, towards the wall of windows that looked out onto the famous skyline. The sun had started to set, adding a romantic glow to the silhouettes of the Empire State and the Chrysler Building and the cluster of other skyscrapers to the north she couldn't identify.

Get it together, Alison. It's not cynical to be on the pill—it's smart.

She listened to him get off the bed and disappear into the bathroom; the lock clicked.

When he returned a few minutes later, she had managed to drag her exhausted body under the sheets.

He wore a robe, but still the glimpse of washboard abs had the traitorous pheromones skittering back into her tender sex.

But she yawned, as the exhaustion of the flight, and everything that had happened since she had arrived, began to claim her.

'You should get some sleep,' he said, but the suggestion seemed strangely impersonal. 'You can stay in here and I'll pick one of the other bedrooms.'

What? They weren't going to share a bedroom?

A silly wobble of emotion tightened around her throat, but she didn't protest as she watched him gather a few pieces of clothing from the dresser drawers.

'I'll get the staff to reorganise our belongings tomorrow,' he said.

'You don't have to give up your bedroom,' she said, feeling stupidly bereft.

'Not a problem,' he said. Then strode back to the bed, leant down and kissed her forehead. The wobble intensified. 'Make yourself at home,' he added. 'Manny the doorman can order you in any food you want—just dial zero on the interlink. He can also arrange a car and driver if you want to go sightseeing or shopping tomorrow.'

'You won't be here?' she asked, then wanted to bite back the suggestion because it made her sound needy, and clingy. And she'd never been either.

'I'm going to be busy with the deal negotiations until tomorrow night... I'll see you back here at seven when the clerk is due and then to escort you to...' he paused '...whatever event we're supposed to be seen at.'

'The opening of the Claxton Gallery?' she said, because she'd memorised the schedule Selene had given her.

Stupidly she'd been looking forward to spending the next twenty-four hours with him, getting to know him a little better, because there had been nothing on the schedule. She realised the foolishness of that supposition, though. He was a busy man, and his business came first. He was certainly under no obligation to entertain her while she was here.

'On the Upper East Side? At eight?' she added, because his face had gone blank, his gaze dipping down to the place where her fingers clutched the sheet over her breasts.

His head lifted. '*Oui*—that.' His smile seemed tight and a little strained, and she wasn't sure he had even heard her, but still the wry tilt of his lips helped the breath to release from her lungs. 'Will you be okay on your own?' he asked.

'Yes, of course,' she said. 'Terrific.'

But as he left the room, the wobble became a wave.

CHAPTER SEVEN

'HI. IT'S ALISON, isn't it?'

Ally swung round from the lavish buffet laid out against the raw redbrick wall of the stark modernist art gallery to find a beautiful and heavily pregnant woman—her plate already laden with delicacies—smiling at her.

'Yes, it's Alison, although everyone calls me Ally,' she said.

'Everyone except your new husband.' The woman's smile became sweetly conspiratorial. 'It's very hot the way Dominic calls you Alison in that French accent. Sorry, I should introduce myself. My name's Megan De Rossi—I'm Dario De Rossi's wife. De Rossi Corp were one of Dominic's early investors when he moved LN's main offices to New York a few years ago.' She offered her hand. 'Which means I've basically been abandoned too—because my husband and your husband have been talking shop ever since we arrived.'

Ally took Megan's hand, feeling hideously exposed by the woman's relaxed, friendly manner. She'd never felt less like Dominic's wife. Other than their marriage ceremony—which had been dealt with in a few short sentences—they had hardly spoken to each other since yesterday evening.

Not since their mind-blowing session to seal their marriage bargain. When he'd treated her as if she were a particularly sumptuous treat that deserved to be savoured and devoured at the same time—then abandoned her.

The memory of their lovemaking and his abrupt departure had kept her awake in the huge king-size bed most of the night. And she'd been obsessing about it most of the day while she took the car and driver Dominic had insisted she use to do some window-shopping in the fashion boutiques of the East Village.

Dominic had appeared at the same time as the clerk to complete the marraige and escort her to this event as scheduled an hour ago, but since the perfunctory ceremony, he'd barely spoken to her—far too busy typing on his phone.

She'd felt his eyes on her when she'd stood beside him in front of the clerk, but no compliment on her outfit had been forthcoming like the last time. And her enquiries during their ride over about how the deal negotiations were going had elicited one-syllable replies.

During the silent, tense ride in the limo, a thousand and one questions had spun through her mind—had she done something wrong, messed up somehow? But she'd forced herself to bury her insecurities deep.

This deal was important and he was obviously preoccupied. Not everything was about her.

So she'd remained silent during the ride. And when they'd arrived, she'd been far too affected by his nearness, warm and solid and overwhelming when he had taken her arm and held her close—as any besotted newly-wed would—as they'd run the gauntlet of reporters and press photographers outside the event, to breathe let alone speak.

As soon as they were safely inside, he'd introduced her to a couple of the consortium members who were attending the event—but once the conversation had moved on to the intricacies of the deal, which was clearly still being negotiated, she had known she was surplus to requirements and had excused herself by explaining she was keen to look at the art.

She'd been miserable ever since—feeling like the class geek who had been invited to the birthday party of the most popular girl in school by mistake. Everyone else here seemed to know each other, drinking and chatting and laughing and mingling to their hearts' content. Ally had stood in the corner, and watched them, trying not to go over and over in her head all the things she hadn't had the guts to ask Dominic in the car.

Being a trophy wife was so much tougher than it looked.

'I thought I'd come and join you,' Megan added. 'I hope you don't mind.'

'Not at all,' Ally said, stifling her discomfort. She knew of Megan De Rossi—she was an important influencer on the New York social scene, not just because her husband was a billionaire but because she ran a ground-breaking charity to help women trapped in abusive relationships and she was the daughter of Alexis Whittaker, a famous British It-Girl of yesteryear. What Ally hadn't expected was the other woman's thoughtfulness—having spotted Ally looking like a lost cat, she had come over to rescue her.

'When is your baby due?' Ally asked, hoping to direct the conversation away from the subject of their 'husbands'.

Megan smiled as she stroked a hand over the prodigious baby bump. An odd shaft of envy pierced Ally's chest.

'Not baby, as it turns out, but *babies*.' Megan laughed. 'Dario and I got the shock news four months ago and we're still adjusting to it. I'm actually only six months, even though I'm the size of an elephant. The two of them, both boys, are not due until June.'

'Twin boys!' Ally grinned, she couldn't help it, impressed by the other woman's *sangfroid*. 'Wow, that… That must be exciting…and terrifying.'

'Right on both counts.' Megan grinned back. 'Although the most terrifying thing so far has been explaining to our daughter Issy she's going to have two more younger brothers when she's not that impressed with the one she's got. Our only consolation is that my sister Katie, who is also due in June, discovered she's having a girl.'

'I'm sure your daughter will get over it,' Ally said, feeling stupidly envious now. 'It's so much better to have siblings than not, even if they are brothers!'

'Precisely, although Issy's not convinced.' Megan popped a delicate mini quiche into her mouth and swallowed. 'But enough about me. I wanted to come over and congratulate you on your marriage. I always knew Dominic would eventually find a woman worth keeping. He certainly seemed to be looking hard enough,' she added with a laugh.

'Thank you, I think.' Ally's heart wrestled with her tonsils at Megan's smile—if she could joke about Dominic like this they must be good friends, although he hadn't mentioned Megan, or anyone else. Embarrassed colour rushed into her cheeks as she realised how little she knew about her brand-new husband's private life.

'And I also wanted to discover where you bought that dress.' Megan's gaze slid over the cocktail dress Ally had spent the afternoon finishing while she'd waited for Dominic to arrive.

An above-the-knee design of aquamarine silk, inspired by a waterfall she'd seen once in a magazine, the dress was all flowing lines and quiet power. The gold band round her biceps had seemed like the perfect finishing touch. But Ally had been second-guessing her decision to wear it as soon as she'd arrived. Was it too revealing? Too funky? Not formal enough?

'It's so original and stylish,' Megan said. 'You look incredible in it.'

The flush of pleasure at Megan De Rossi's heartfelt praise had Ally's ribs contracting. This was exactly the kind of feedback she had hoped for.

'Actually I made it myself,' she said.

Megan's eyes widened, but then she whistled. 'That's even more amazing. You're really talented. I've never seen anything so cool and distinctive.'

Ally's heart squeezed. She'd hoped for a reaction like this, but she hadn't expected it.

'You're nothing like Dominic's other girlfriends—no wonder he decided to marry you,' Megan added, making the blush fire across Ally's chest. 'And that's without even factoring in that super-hot kiss,' Megan finished, her grin becoming decidedly wicked.

Ally's blush went ballistic.

Photos of their kiss on the sidewalk had hit

the Internet yesterday. Ally knew because she'd been inundated with messages from her friends in London asking to know what the heck was going on. But she hadn't replied and she'd studiously avoided social media all day.

'I'm sorry,' Megan said, immediately looking contrite. 'I didn't mean to embarrass you. But, honestly, you two looked amazing together. So hot and so much in love, if anyone thought he shouldn't have ditched Mira they certainly won't after seeing that photo. Was that amazing blue suit one of your designs, too?'

'Yes,' Ally croaked, quietly dying inside.

She'd known she would have to lie, but she hadn't realised it would be quite this hard.

She already liked Megan De Rossi. The woman was smart, and witty, and sweet and surprisingly down to earth. And she clearly had exceptional taste. Megan and she might have become friends, if her marriage to Dominic had been real, instead of a subterfuge to secure a property deal.

'Um…' Ally began, not sure what to say, when she was rescued by a tall man in a dark grey designer suit, who swooped down on them like an avenging angel.

'Damn it, what are you doing on your feet? And holding something so heavy, *piccola*.' He whisked the laden plate Megan had been nibbling on out of her hand.

This was Dario De Rossi, Ally realised, in the flesh. She'd seen his picture in magazines, but it didn't do him justice. He was a strikingly handsome man, his Italian heritage evident in the black hair, olive skin, phenomenal bone structure—and his wildly overprotective manner.

'You are carrying two babies. *My* babies. You need to sit down, *piccola*,' he said, cradling his wife's elbow to lead her to a chair.

'And *you* need to stop calling me *piccola* now I'm the size of a house.' Megan rolled her eyes comically but allowed herself to be led. 'Ally, meet Dario—my very own papa bear. Dario, this is Ally, Dominic's new wife.'

Having deposited Megan on one of the white leather couches that lined the stark walls of the art gallery, and handed the plate back to her, Dario offered Ally his hand.

'Ally, it is good to meet you. I have heard much about you from Dominic.'

You have?

Ally shook his hand, wondering what on earth Dominic could have found to say about her, seeing as he hardly knew her. The firm handshake settled her nerves a fraction, until Dario shouted at someone.

'Dominic, over here.' He beckoned over Ally's shoulder, then smiled down at her. 'Your husband has been searching for you, like a besotted newly-wed.'

He has? But he isn't a besotted newly-wed.

Before Ally had a chance to process why Dominic might *really* have been searching for her, a large hand settled on the small of her back, burning the sensitive skin through the silk. She tried not to jump, not to overreact to the sensuous caress as Dominic's palm coasted to her hip and dragged her to his side.

'There you are, Alison,' he murmured in her ear, very much like an attentive lover but she could hear the edge in his voice. Something wasn't right.

'Megan, Dario, this is my *wife*, Alison,' he said, the possessive tone sending an inappropriate shaft of heat to her sex.

Fabulous, Ally, even his temper has the ability to turn you on.

'We've met,' Megan chipped in after swallowing another mouthful from her plate. 'And for once I approve, Dominic. Your bride is amazing,' she added, sending Ally a conspiratorial wink.

'Merci beaucoup,' Dominic murmured, dryly.

'Although I'm not sure you deserve her,' Megan added.

'I'm sure I do not,' Dominic replied, the tone deliberately self-deprecating but Ally could still hear that edge, even if Megan couldn't.

She had definitely screwed up somehow. Not acted quite dutiful or besotted enough, maybe?

'I can't believe you didn't at least mention in your press release about the marriage that Ally is a talented fashion designer,' Megan said.

Ally tensed at the innocuous comment as Dominic's hand jerked on her hip. Oh, crap. She hadn't expected Megan to blurt that out.

'By the way, I forgot to ask where your designs retail,' Megan asked her, caressing her baby bump. 'I can't wait to check them out, as soon as I get rid of these two and loose the five hundred extra pounds I've managed to put on.'

'Stop.' Dario cupped her cheek. 'You are not fat. You are pregnant and beautiful.'

'Spoken like a man who isn't carrying around five hundred extra pounds,' Megan said, but covered his hand with hers in a gesture that made Ally's heart leap into her throat.

What must that be like? To have a man be devoted to you? Exciting? Scary? She had no idea.

Dominic's hand had tightened on her waist. Whatever had annoyed him already, he was clearly a lot more annoyed now.

Why hadn't she told him she was making her own wardrobe for this trip?

'What designs?' he said.

His jaw had hardened. Okay, he wasn't just annoyed, he was *really* annoyed. And no wonder—she'd just potentially exposed what a sham their marriage was to two of his friends. She should have kept her mouth shut about the dress to Megan until she'd had the guts to admit she'd made it herself to Dominic.

'I need to go to the ladies' room,' she said, hoping to escape and defuse the situation. But he held her in place.

'What designs is Megan talking about?' The sharp frown made heat prickle over her skin.

She could feel Megan's and Dario's gazes on the two of them.

'Can we talk about this later?' she whispered. Surely he wasn't going to flip out in front of his friends—wouldn't that blow their cover completely? But he seemed unconcerned by their audience when he placed his free hand on her other hip and tugged her to face him.

'*What* designs, Alison?' he repeated, the tone broaching no more argument or prevarication.

'I… I made some of my own clothes for this trip,' she said.

'You didn't know?' She heard Megan's gasped question, but all Ally's focus was on Dominic now. On his reaction. Because his brows had lowered ominously.

I'm so sorry, I should have told you, but don't make a big deal of it or we'll both be totally busted.

She tried to communicate the desperate plea to him telepathically.

'Which clothes?' he said, not picking up on her frantic telecommunications.

'Well…' Colour burned her cheeks as his gaze roamed over the dress—in much the same way as it had when he'd recited his vows earlier.

'Tell me,' he said, stroking her hips now,

making the soft silk feel like sandpaper as it rasped over her skin.

'All of them.'

He swore softly, let go of her hips and grasped her hand. 'We're leaving.'

Panic assailed her as she heard Megan's shouted comment. 'Where are you going?'

'I have to *talk* to my wife.' Dominic threw the comment over his shoulder.

Ally attempted to wave her new friend good-bye, but she was already being whisked through the crowd. People turned to watch as she was marched out of the gallery. Some of the women giggled behind their hands, a few of the men laughed, others simply stared at the spectacle they were making or lifted their phones to record her humiliation.

Ally allowed herself to be led; trying to resist would only make the situation worse. He was furious, obviously. It was the only explanation for the sparkle of heat in his eyes, the tight line of his jaw, the way his hand clasped hers in a firm, unyielding grip.

She should never have designed and made her own clothes, instead of buying them from somewhere expensive and exclusive the way he'd expected her to. He was a proud man and this marriage was all about appearances. She had miscalculated badly. Very badly.

Stopping on the sidewalk outside the gallery, he whistled through his fingers. The limousine they'd arrived in appeared out of the snarl of traffic like a magic carpet.

'I'm sorry, Dominic, I should have told you, about the clothes,' she whispered, trying to placate him. 'I realise you're probably annoyed that I didn't buy something from a named designer, but I've been studying design for two years and I—'

'Get in.' Dominic opened the door and held it for her.

She hesitated.

'Alison. Get. In. The. Damn. Car.' The tone was low, more firm than threatening, but still she felt it ripple down her spine. *'Now.'*

She jumped at the barked command, and slid into the seat. Moments later she was cocooned in the back of the car with him as it peeled away from the kerb. The scent of leather and man, spicy cologne and pine soap invaded her senses; the blare of car horns, the cacophony of sound from the street as New York woke up to the night buzzed in her brain, combining with the sensation careering over her skin.

Why was he so mad at her? And why did it still turn her on?

'Listen, I'm really sorry I wasn't honest with you about my wardrobe. But Megan liked this dress, really, it isn't all bad—'

'Stop apologising about the damn dress. The dress is not the problem. It's stunning, and it's been driving me to distraction ever since I saw you in it. So I'd say Megan's opinion is correct.' The searing confession surprised her so much, the bottom dropped out of her stomach.

'Then… What is the problem?' Because there was clearly a problem and she still had no idea what it was.

He turned to her then, the naked hunger on his face so shocking the heat fired up her torso. 'The problem is, for this to work there has to be trust. You chose not to tell me about the clothes, and in some ways I understand that— you're obviously not as confident about your abilities as you should be.' His hand touched her thigh and she shivered, the sensation both brutal and yet delicious as the calluses trailed up her leg. 'Which is ironic, because the minute I saw you in this outfit tonight, all I wanted to do was rip it off you.'

'I'm not sure that's relevant,' she managed because she'd already started to lose the thread of this conversation, and she was still none the wiser as to why he looked so furious.

He swore suddenly and let her go, to lean back in his seat. 'Then it should be,' he said, staring out of the window.

She wondered if she should apologise again, for not telling him about the clothes, because it had upset him in ways she hadn't thought she could upset him, but she didn't want to keep apologising.

The ride through Manhattan seemed to take an eternity as she waited for him to say something, anything. Her thigh quivered where the imprint of his brief caress still lingered—making her brutally aware of exactly how tangled this situation had become. Because she still wanted him so desperately, even though on several levels he was completely infuriating.

Her need and her anxiety had reached fever pitch when he finally turned back to her.

'Why did you have Selene cut the one-million-pound payment from the divorce settlement?' he said tightly, the searing heat in his eyes accompanied by an emotion that made no sense whatsoever.

Guilt.

That was the problem? She opened her mouth to reply, but then closed it again, because she still didn't understand what she'd done that was so wrong.

'Answer me,' Dominic demanded. He was so angry and frustrated he was finding it hard to speak. He'd trusted her and she'd tricked him.

Hold it together. And don't touch her, damn it, because then you'll never be able to get an answer.

Her eyes had gone wide with confusion. Making the fury boiling under his breastbone threaten to ignite.

He'd only found out about the contract change a half-hour ago, when he'd been scanning an email from Selene while waiting to pick up a glass of champagne for Alison at the event's crowded bar.

He'd been planning to celebrate. And he'd wanted to celebrate with her. The consortium members had been completely charmed by her, as he'd known they would be. She'd put on a convincing show, not least by excusing herself when his introductions had led on to a discussion about zoning issues on the project. One of the businessmen had laughed and congratulated him on his marriage and his beautiful wife, pointing out, 'Only a real wife would feel comfortable making it abundantly clear she found her husband's talk of business boring. My wife is exactly the same.'

The consortium members had agreed to sign the first phase of the deal tomorrow morning. His decision to marry Alison had been the right move.

But then he'd read Selene's outline of the marriage-contract negotiations, and the excitement had died. His assistant hadn't bothered to mention the change Alison had requested before now, because he'd given Selene *carte blanche* to negotiate the terms, telling her to refer anything problematic to his legal and financial teams. He hadn't wanted to be too closely involved. He'd been having enough trouble forgetting about Alison while he'd waited for her to arrive in New York. And, of course, his legal and financial teams had been more than happy to strike the lump-sum payment at the end of the marriage from the contract, because it would save LN a million pounds.

But he wasn't happy. He was furious about the unnecessary change.

The whole purpose of the payment was to keep his conscience clear. To pay off his responsibility after the marriage ended, not just towards the woman whose virginity he had taken, however unintentionally, and then exploited, but also towards the little girl who had been left destitute after that summer.

By refusing that payment, she had turned the tables on him. Made him responsible again. And guilt was not an emotion he enjoyed.

'I just… I didn't want the money,' she said. 'It was too much. You're already giving me so much.'

It was exactly the sort of naïve, artless statement he should have expected. He tried to bank his fury. But he could do nothing to hide his frustration.

'We agreed on the money the morning you agreed to this marriage. And then you deliberately reneged on that understanding. And you chose not to mention it before we actually went through with the ceremony. Why?'

'I didn't think you'd mind,' she said, still confused, which only spurred his temper more.

'Of course I mind,' he said. 'I always pay my debts. It's an important principle of the way I do business.' And something he'd stuck to throughout his career, even when it had meant going hungry. Because he had promised himself the night he had crawled off his father's estate he would never, ever be beholden to anyone again. That no one would ever have the power to control him in that way. And now this woman had managed to undermine that essential tenet to the way he lived his life—without even trying.

'Why did you even wish to change that part of the agreement?' he said. He had offered her a million pounds; why hadn't she taken it? Because he knew exactly how much she could use the money.

Her blush was visible even in the dark interior of the car.

'It's too much, Dominic.'

'No. It. Isn't.' He spat the words out. 'You're going to live as my wife for the next six months—

do you really think I want to leave you destitute again when we divorce?' And why was it already so damn hard to say that word?

She looked shocked, which only infuriated him more. He couldn't let this pass.

The car drew up at the Lafayette apartment. He unbuckled them both and hauled Alison out of the car. She still hadn't said anything, but it was probably better they had this discussion in private. He didn't want to risk another display for the paparazzi out on the sidewalk.

He marched into the lobby, ignored Manny the doorman's jaunty evening greeting and stabbed the elevator button.

Unfortunately a couple of his staff arrived behind them, and joined them in the lift.

Her fingers flexed on his, but he didn't release his grip as he replied to his staff members' innocuous comments about the weather—even as the adrenaline raced through his bloodstream. How could he still be so aroused, when he was almost choking on his indignation?

At last the two employees stepped out of the lift and they arrived a few moments later at the penthouse apartment. He dragged her through the doors as soon as they swished open. Once they were safe in the privacy of his apartment he released her hand.

'I want to know why you pulled this stunt,' he said. 'And then we're going to have to re-negotiate the contract or it's not going to work for me.'

CHAPTER EIGHT

WAS IT WRONG to notice how hot Dominic was when he was mad?

Ally tried to corral her wayward thoughts and stick to the problem at hand.

And it was a problem. She should have told him she'd decided not to accept the pay-off. That much was obvious. But she really hadn't thought it would be a deal breaker. And she had to wonder why it was.

But she was going to have to give him an answer first. An answer that would expose all her insecurities. Which was probably why she hadn't told him in the first place.

But the truth was, she'd already told him the reason; he just hadn't been listening. So now she would have to tell him again.

'I couldn't get past what happened to my mother with your father. Accepting your money felt like I was making the same mistake. She persuaded herself she loved him. But I'm not sure she ever really did. What she loved was the security his money provided. I don't want to sell myself short the way she did.'

'This deal, this marriage, hasn't got a damn thing to do with what happened all those years ago. We already established that.' The edge in his voice sharpened.

'Yes, it does. I won't compromise myself like that. I can't.'

'So you expect me to compromise my integrity instead,' he shot back.

'What?' she asked, because she was confused now as well as heartsore. She hadn't meant to cause an argument. And she certainly didn't want to infuriate him. But she couldn't budge on this. She'd tried and she just couldn't; her pride wouldn't allow her to accept the money. 'I don't... I don't understand.'

'Really?' he said, thrusting his fingers through his hair. 'Then let me explain. You don't want to be like your mother, but you're happy to make me into my father. To have me exploit you the way my father exploited her and hundreds of other women. The way he exploited my own mother. If you don't want to be like her, what makes you think I want to be like him?'

It didn't make any sense. This had nothing to do with his father. Far from it. But from his tortured expression it was obvious it mattered to him.

'But you're not exploiting me, Dominic,' she said, as patiently and gently as she could— she needed to defuse this situation and make him see sense. 'I want to be here. I signed that contract and went through with the ceremony earlier in full knowledge of the facts. I just don't want the money. It's too much. You're not responsible for what happened to my mother. They were the grown-ups, not you.'

'*Mon Dieu.* How do you know what I am responsible for when you don't even know what happened that night?'

The growled admission struck her like a blow. Bringing back the memories she had never really confronted. And the words her mother had whispered before dragging her out of bed in the middle of the night, her cheek bruised and her eyes wet with tears, returned.

'*Something terrible's happened, baby. Pierre's very angry with me and Dominic. We have to leave.*'

'What are you saying, Dominic?' A horrible

thought curdled in the pit of her stomach. Had something happened between her mother and Dominic? The thought had never even occurred to her. Because it would be ludicrous and paranoid—but a stifling coating of jealousy joined the snakes writhing in her belly, regardless.

Which only disturbed her more. Imagine being jealous of a dead woman. A woman who was her own mother.

He swore and turned away from her, striding to the open-plan kitchen and pulling a beer out of the fridge. He snapped off the cap against the countertop and gulped down half the bottle.

She followed him, her insides churning. A part of her had always wondered what had happened to turn Pierre against her mother. But it couldn't be this, could it?

'Did Pierre catch you together?' she asked.

Had her mother seduced a sixteen-year-old boy? The thought was so appalling she knew she would never be able to get past it. She had clung to that last modicum of respect for her mother for so long—through the drug addiction, the endless affairs with increasingly inappropriate men. But this would destroy the last of it. And be worse than anything she'd been forced to witness her mother do in the years after that night.

'Is that why he hit her?' she asked. 'Why he kicked us out? Did you and my mother have a relationship?'

But as she steeled herself against hearing the worst, Dominic choked on the beer and the bottle slammed down on the countertop.

'What the…? Are you…? How do you say it in English?' he said, the frustration hitting boiling point. 'Are you insane?' he managed. 'Of course I didn't have a relationship with *Monique.*'

The stabbing pain in Ally's belly unlocked. *Oh, thank God.* Her mother hadn't done the unthinkable and seduced a child.

'I was only sixteen and your mother was in her thirties, stunningly beautiful and in love with my father. Even I was never that precocious,' he said, sounding so shocked she felt pretty foolish for even thinking it might have been a possibility, let alone actually asking him. But she was still glad she had. She never wanted that ugly picture in her head ever again. And now at least it was gone… But if that wasn't what had caused his father to hit her mother, what had? And why would Dominic feel responsible?

'But you were there, when Pierre hit her?' she asked. He must have been. Because her mother had mentioned him and he had just implied as much. 'Do you know why he hurt her? Why he turned on her?'

His gaze became shuttered, but not before she caught the flash of something that looked like regret.

He braced his hands against the countertop and dropped his head. She could see the tension in the rigid line of his shoulder blades, and hear the deep sigh as his chest released.

'There was no reason,' he said, but she could hear the bitterness that he couldn't disguise. 'My father never needed a reason. His temper was volatile and easily roused. I think your mother made some innocuous comment about their engagement. And he exploded.'

'I see.' Ally's chest deflated, his agonised words, the description of what he'd witnessed, having the hideous ring of truth. 'So he *had* offered her marriage?' she whispered.

Dominic's head lifted, and he nodded. 'Of course, it was how my father liked to operate. Dangle the carrot and then apply the stick.'

Ally's heart shrank in her chest.

Dominic gulped down the last of the beer. And dumped the empty bottle in the trash. He looked exhausted. As exhausted as she felt. She noticed the scar bisecting his left eyebrow, the scar she'd wondered about often as a child.

He liked to dangle the carrot, then apply the stick.

His statement stirred the memories again, of all the altercations she'd witnessed between father and son that summer. The bullying, the insults, the constant, endless attempts by Pierre to let his son know he was a bastard, that he wasn't enough.

As a child she'd been in awe of Pierre, the way her mother had. Because he'd always been so charming to her, she'd never been able to figure out why he was so mean to Dominic. But now she could see, Pierre had treated her like a pet that summer, not a daughter. And a tool, his praise for her just one more stick to beat Dominic with, to let him know that even his mistress's child had a greater place in Pierre's affections than his illegitimate son.

'I'm sorry,' she said. 'For bringing it up, for making you relive that summer and those events.'

His eyes met hers, the confusion in them as compelling as the wariness. Dominic, she thought, was not a man comfortable with displays of emotion, or affection—no wonder this evening had exhausted him.

But even so she refused to hold back. Reaching across the breakfast bar, she placed her palm on his cheek, trying to soothe the bone-deep exhaustion she could see in his eyes.

'And I'm sorry for thinking, even for a moment, you were to blame for the horrid way my mother and I were treated at the end of that summer, when it was always, always him.'

Dominic tensed, and jerked his head back, away from the soft stroke of her fingers.

The compassion and understanding in her eyes horrified him almost as much as the desire to lean into the caress. To take whatever solace she offered.

She dropped her hand, and tensed, as if his rejection were a physical blow.

But he didn't deserve her sympathy, or her apology. She didn't know the full extent of what had happened that night—that his father wasn't the only one to blame.

But he had absolutely no intention of telling her.

It was ancient history now. And it had no bearing on who they were now. And on their marriage.

One thing was clear, though: despite everything that had happened to Alison, and however much she might think she was as cynical and pragmatic about this relationship as he was because of those struggles—she wasn't. Some of that hopeful, generous, open-hearted child still remained. Or she would never have believed his explanation about that night so easily, been so ready to absolve him. And she certainly would not have refused to take the one million pounds he'd offered her.

Walking round the breakfast bar, he cupped her chin, pulled her head up. 'I don't want to talk about the past again. It is dead and has been for a long time.'

It was a brutal thing to say, especially when he saw the humiliating colour fire into her cheeks. But he had to be cruel to be kind now, or she would invest too much of herself in this relationship.

'You must take the money,' he said again. 'For this arrangement to work.'

She tugged her chin out of his hand, looked down at her clasped hands, the knuckles white with strain.

He waited for her to accept the inevitable. She had to know he was giving her an ultimatum.

When she lifted her head all he could see in her eyes was an aching sadness—and even though he didn't feel particularly triumphant, he thought he had won.

But then she shook her head and to his astonishment she said, 'I can't, Dominic. I just can't. If that means we have to part, then I'll understand.'

He was so shocked, the riot of emotions flowing through him so strong and so new—panic, fear, regret, but most of all loss—he had no idea how to process them, let alone how to combat them.

'Non,' he said. Placing his hands on her cheeks,

he drew her face towards his. Before he could think better of the impulse, he covered her mouth with his. He wasn't going to lose her; he couldn't.

She opened for him and he plunged his tongue into the recesses of her mouth. Taking, demanding, possessing her—refusing to accept her stubbornness, her intransigence.

The deal. The deal required she stay. That was the reason he felt so desperate. The reason the yearning was so intense. It had to be.

Her instant and unequivocal surrender was like a drug. Sex would fix this problem.

The blood rushed to his groin as he lifted her into his arms and carried her towards his old bedroom. The one she'd chosen the day before.

This is madness. She knows this is madness. We don't have to end this over something so foolish. As long as I can prove she still wants me too. That's all that really matters here.

He placed her on her feet, held her waist and looked into amber eyes, dark with arousal. 'We can fix this in the morning,' he said, his voice hoarse. He would figure out a way if it killed him. 'But for now I want to do what we do best.'

It wasn't really a question but she nodded anyway. And his heart leapt in his chest.

This isn't over. Not yet.

Yes, I want you. I want this. I don't want to leave.

The heat plunged low in Ally's abdomen, rebounding in her sex.

Just take me to bed and let's forget, for tonight at least.

She shuddered, her body alive with too much sensation, as his hands skimmed over her bottom and lifted her dress. He dragged her into his embrace, until the thick evidence of his desire rubbed against the soft, liquid warmth flooding between her thighs.

She didn't see how they could fix this. But for now all she wanted to do was feel, because it might be her last chance.

His thumbs edged under the legs of her panties. He cupped her bottom in hard hands.

'I can't go slowly. Is that okay?' he asked, his voice full of an urgency that only made her more desperate.

'Yes,' she said, her sex already clutching and

releasing, desperate to feel that thick length inside her, one last time.

'Bien.' He found the hammering pulse in her neck with firm lips.

She clung to him, trying to dispel the fear, and the sadness.

She jumped at the sound of rending fabric as he ripped away her panties, and her senses soared. The turmoil of emotions forgotten, as giddy shock became giddy excitement.

He turned her round and bent her over the bed.

Her thighs quivered as she heard him release himself from his pants. Large hands positioned her, skimming over her hips, brushing her bottom, then the huge head of his erection notched at the slick seam of her sex.

She jerked, shocked by the need coursing through her like wild fire as he impaled her in one slow thrust.

'Always so wet for me, Madame LeGrand,' he said, but the tone sounded rough, and raw.

She groaned as he filled her to the hilt, the penetration from this angle so deep what had been overwhelming before became devastating.

He began to rock, out and back, going deeper,

taking more. She gripped the coverlet, trying to anchor herself for the heavy thrusts, trying to control the depth of penetration. Her muscles contracted, pushing her towards that high wide ledge, but his movements only became more frantic, the pleasure refusing to subside.

His thumb found her swollen clitoris, sending her soaring, shattering, flying again. Her shocked sobs matched his deep guttural groans.

One large callused palm found her breast, ripping away the silk of her dress, the confining lace of her bra, until hot skin found hot skin. Freed, the stiff peak engorged under his relentless caresses, driving her even higher as he sank deeper and deeper inside her.

The sound of sex, graphic and basic, the cries of pleasure and passion, filled the room, the sensations dazzling and disorientating.

She crashed over one final time and fell to earth. He grew even larger inside her, the hot seed pumping into her as he shouted out his fulfilment.

She collapsed onto the bed.

The shaking began as he eased out of her.

'Are you okay?' he said, his gruff voice rippling through her in the darkness.

'Yes,' she said, because she was, even though the thought of having to leave him tomorrow was crucifying her.

She rolled over and sat up, gathering the torn bodice of her dress, feeling suddenly defence-less. Scared to look at him. Scared not to.

'I damaged your beautiful gown,' he said. 'Can it be repaired?'

'It's okay,' she said. 'I can make another. I like to do it,' she added, because he looked a little dazed. She knew the feeling. How could the sex be so powerful, so overwhelming, so right, when everything else seemed so wrong?

He nodded. 'We will talk tomorrow morning. And work this disagreement out,' he said.

The sadness settled back over her body, dispelling the golden glow of the orgasms he'd given her. But she nodded. Prepared to pretend she believed it.

'I'll see you in the morning,' he said.

'Yes,' she said.

She wanted to snag his wrist, to ask him to stay, to sleep with her, to hold her, just this once, but she knew that indulgence would only make tomorrow harder.

So instead she watched him leave the room.

Then dropped back on the bed and blinked furiously, to stop the tears she wanted to shed from falling.

Their marriage had been legal for approximately three hours. And already it felt so much more real than it should. Which was why she couldn't give in and accept the money.

She had to preserve her independence, and this was the only way she could think of to do it, because it would be far, far too easy to surrender everything to this man. Not just her body, but also her soul.

While all the time knowing he would never be willing to surrender more than his body in return.

CHAPTER NINE

FEVERISH THOUGHTS CIRCLED Ally's brain as she showered and dressed the next morning. It was past nine o'clock when she stepped into the apartment's living room feeling as if she were about to step into the abyss.

Dominic sat at the breakfast bar eating a bagel and scrolling through what she suspected were market reports on his phone.

He put the bagel down and wiped his mouth when he spotted her.

'*Bonjour*, Alison.'

She drew in a breath and forced herself to walk towards him. Even dressed in jeans and a T-shirt, his feet bare and his damp hair slicked back from his forehead, he looked indomitable and unreachable.

Her heart sank. She'd gone over all the possible solutions she could think of to their problem and she couldn't see one. She couldn't take the money, and Dominic would not accept her refusal.

'Don't look so worried,' he murmured as he held out his hand. 'I have an idea that will satisfy me and I hope will also satisfy you.'

She placed her fingers in his palm, felt the familiar frisson of electricity as he grasped her hand and directed her to the stool next to him.

'I still can't accept the money,' she said, scared that his solution would involve going over the same ground as yesterday.

'And I cannot accept leaving you destitute when we part.'

She wouldn't be destitute, but it was pointless arguing about it once more.

'Then we're at an impasse.' She blinked furiously, pathetically close to tears, again. Why was she about to cry?

His intransigence, his unwillingness to bend on a point that was so important to her, surely proved this arrangement had always been doomed to failure.

'Not necessarily.' His lips curved in a persuasive smile. 'How about, rather than giving you a million pounds at the end of this marriage, I invest in your business instead?'

'What business?' she asked, completely non-plussed.

'Your fashion design business, of course,' he said.

'But I don't have a fashion design business.'

'This is exactly the point. You don't have one, but you should.' His gaze slid over the short dress she had put on, ready to return to London on the next plane. He touched the flounced neckline. 'This is one of your designs, is it not?'

She nodded, brutally aware of the approval in his eyes.

'You are extremely talented. Even I can see this and I know nothing about fashion. Megan De Rossi does and she agrees with me. She asked where your designs were retailing yesterday at the gallery, is this not so?'

'That was just a casual comment,' she said. 'She was being kind and friendly.'

'No, she wasn't, because I phoned her an hour ago and asked her if she would be willing to throw her support behind your brand.'

'You did...*what*?' Ally jumped off the stool. 'Dominic, how could you?' She covered her face with her hands, wishing the beautiful concrete floor of his apartment would crack open and swallow her whole.

His fingers curled around her wrists and he drew her hands away from her face. He peered at her, the smile so confident now it was verging on smug. 'Don't you want to hear what she said?'

'No! I don't.' She yanked her hands free, not sure whether she wanted to shout at him or simply curl up in a ball and weep. 'She's your friend, and you put her on the spot. I have no doubt she was polite.' She stepped away from him.

How would she ever survive the humiliation?

Megan De Rossi had been wonderful. And for that bright beautiful moment when the other woman had admired her design yesterday, Ally had felt as if she belonged, truly belonged. But it had all been an illusion. An illusion that Dominic had shattered with careless disregard for her feelings.

'You've exposed me to ridicule, Dominic. Can't you see that? I haven't even finished fashion college yet. I've got months of work left before my final year show. And then, if none of the fashion houses are interested, it could be years before I manage to get an internship. They're hugely competitive and I don't even know if I've got what it takes to—'

'Megan wants to invest,' he interrupted her, his smile not smug so much as sympathetic.

'What?' What on earth was he talking about now?

'Megan De Rossi wants to invest in your brand, *ma belle*,' he said again, chuckling as he grasped both her wrists again and tugged her struggling body back towards him, until she was positioned between his thighs. 'She loves your designs. She says you have huge potential. I told her I was considering bankrolling your collection. I asked her for her advice, whether she thought it would be a good investment. I didn't want to suggest something that would not succeed. She not only said it would be a fabulous investment, she said she wanted to invest, too.'

'She…she didn't.' Ally's body went limp, the shock making her knees tremble. Megan De Rossi had liked her designs enough to invest in them? It didn't even seem possible, let alone plausible. This was huge. It was beyond huge. It was… Everything.

'She did,' he said. Resting his hand on her neck, he rubbed his thumb across her collarbone where her pulse was pounding like a jackhammer. 'Why are you so surprised?'

'Because...' The tears that she had refused to shed yesterday made her throat raw, and her eyes sting. 'Because it's... It's like a dream come true.'

Dominic tucked a knuckle under her chin, the glitter of unshed tears destroying him. He'd wanted to find a solution to the problem of the money; it seemed he'd found much more than that.

How could he not have realised how insecure she was? Because she'd been so brave and bold and determined up to now—that was why. But underneath that was a woman who had had to fight for every chance, every opportunity, and drag herself through God only knew what to make her dream a reality. Well, she didn't have to drag herself any more. He was going to make sure she soared.

'So, if I said I was going to invest in your start-up, you would accept?'

He saw the dazed hope in her face fade a little. 'But I don't know anything about business. All I know is how to design and make clothes.'

He nodded. This much he could help her with. 'Luckily for you, I know a lot about business,' he said. 'The idea is we would be partners in this venture.' Like a real husband and wife, he thought, but didn't say; he didn't want to spook her, any more than he wanted to spook himself. 'I'll give you all the financial and business support you need. Rent premises in London for your workshop, pay for the salaries of your staff...'

'Staff?' Her eyes went so large he had to resist a laugh.

'Yes, staff. A business manager, a personal assistant, a publicist, and those are just the basics. I would assume a fledgling fashion brand would also need creative staff.'

'But... Isn't that going to be very expensive?' she said and he could already hear her insecurities putting the brakes on her dream.

But he wasn't going to allow it. This was the way he could give her something of value from their marriage. Something that would endure long after their liaison was over. Something that would ensure she would never be destitute again. And he would not have to feel responsible.

'You have to invest money to make money, Alison—that's the way business works.'

'But how will I pay you back?' she asked. And he had to bite his tongue.

He mustn't become frustrated with her, not again. Her insecurity—like his driving ambition—had stemmed from the scars inflicted on both of them that summer. *He* knew she could do this, but she did not, and until she did he would have to be her mentor, her supporter. Gently nudging her in the right direction until each new success showed her how much she could achieve. Confidence didn't happen overnight—confidence had to be built, brick by tortuous brick. He'd discovered that when building his own business, so now he could show her while she built hers.

'You won't pay me back,' he said, but before she could protest he held up his hand. 'Wait, let me explain. The money isn't a gift, or a pay-off, like the alimony payment I was proposing. I intend to get a handsome return on my money, eventually, once the brand is established. We'll make a formal agreement and, for my investment, I want a fifty per cent share of the profits.'

'But what will I be giving to the business that entitles *me* to fifty per cent?' she said, the frown on her face so adorable he wanted to kiss it. 'I haven't got any money to invest in it.'

She really was clueless about how business worked. Why did that make the thought of going into business with her all the more exciting?

'Your contribution is your time and your talent,' he said. 'I'm afraid I'm going to be far too busy with the Waterfront project here to be anything more than a silent partner. And I know absolutely nothing about fashion.'

'But what if I fail?' she said, and his heart cracked at the tremble of uncertainty.

He stifled the foolish feeling of empathy. This was business, just like their marriage, there was no place for sentiment—but even so he kept his voice gentle. 'If you fail, I write the investment off as an expense and reduce my tax burden. Either way, it is a win-win for me financially.'

But she wasn't going to fail. She had the talent, according to Megan, to be a success. The only thing holding her back would be lack of business expertise—which he could supply her with—and her own fear of failure.

And if there was one thing he could show her how to do, it was how to conquer that fear.

'So, what do you say? Do you want to go into business with me, Madame LeGrand?'

She pressed a hand over her breast, as if she were trying to stop her heart jumping out of her chest. He knew how she felt, because he'd felt the same way when he'd signed his first deal with the precious stake he'd earned working round the clock as a cycle courier in Paris.

'I'm terrified,' she said, her honesty so captivating he struggled not to kiss her.

'Only terrified?' he asked.

'And also excited,' she admitted. Hope sparked in her eyes, and found an answering spark in his heart.

'So is that a yes?' he asked, needing the clarification.

'Yes—yes, it is!' she said.

'Magnifique!'

She laughed and grasped his shoulders as he wrapped his arms around her waist and spun her round in a circle.

'Congratulations, Madame LeGrand,' he said

as he finally put her down, absorbing the delicious echo in his groin as her body pressed against his.

'Thank you. Thank you for suggesting this,' she said, her face alight with exhilaration. 'It's a brilliant solution.'

'Yes, I know,' he said, and she laughed again, the sound sweet and carefree.

He slanted his mouth across hers, his pulse pounding in his ears when her eager response turned the kiss from hungry to ravenous in a heartbeat.

He scooped her into his arms.

'Dominic, what are you doing?' she asked, breathlessly as he carried her back into the bedroom.

'Celebrating,' he said, although he thought that much was obvious.

It wasn't till much later though, as he headed down to his offices to get the legal team involved in setting up the new business, while Alison called Megan to talk about coming on board as an investor, that it occurred to him he wasn't even sure what made him smile the most.

The hum in his groin from the celebratory

sex they'd just shared; the thought that the first stage of the Waterfront deal would be signed later today; the realisation he would be able to keep his fake wife, without any regrets; or the thought of the months ahead, when he would be able to help Alison blossom and grow into the woman she was always meant to be—both in bed and in business.

Now they had established trust and secure boundaries to their relationship—ensuring there would be no more messy heart-to-hearts about their feelings or about things that had happened so long ago they no longer mattered—their marriage could progress as originally planned.

They would live separate lives—with Alison busy working on her business in London, while he was engaged in the Waterfront deal in Manhattan.

As he bounded down the emergency stairs to his ninth-floor office, the thought was so enticing, he might even have been whistling.

CHAPTER TEN

'CAN YOU GET them to rethink, Muhammad? We need that Indian silk. It's a key component of the whole collection.' Ally spoke rapidly, her nerves fraying as she opened the gate to the London town house. The smattering of rain permeated the thin sweater she wore. Deciding to walk home this evening hadn't been the smartest idea, but she had wanted some fresh air after a week of eighteen hour days finishing off the designs. Panic constricted around her throat—and now the signature feature of every one might be missing.

She'd fallen in love with the stunning craftsmanship of the embroidered fabric offered by a charitable workshop in Mumbai. She'd been in negotiations with them for weeks—and everything had been going so well, they were due to sign the contracts an hour ago, when she'd got a call from her supplier, Muhammad Patel, with some very bad news.

'They're saying another buyer has promised them a better investment,' her supplier replied. 'I'm sorry, Ally, you've been great and I know they were really torn. Rohana was full of apologies when she told me,' he said, mentioning the workshop's owner who Ally had been dealing with. 'But the other buyer's got more clout in the marketplace.'

Which was code for another designer with an actual name had stepped in and offered, if not more money, then more exposure.

'I understand,' she interrupted him, because she did. 'And please tell Rohana not to feel bad about this. They've got to make the right choice for their business.'

She shoved the phone into her bag, her anxiety threatening to choke her. What had she expected? She didn't have a pedigree, just a rich husband willing to invest in a pipe dream. It had been two months since her deal with Dominic, since she'd started playing businesswoman and pretending to be a fashion designer, and she didn't feel any more secure now than she had then.

Dominic had been wonderful, but he was busy, and she didn't want to bother him about the minutiae of her business problems on the few days a month when she got to see him. After the almost-end to their arrangement a day into the marriage, she'd been determined to stick to her end of the bargain—and to enjoy every second of time she had with him.

The sex had been awesome. The way he could make her body feel was a revelation—the familiar heat blasted through her at the memory of their last merry meeting in Paris a week ago, when he'd had to attend the opening of a rail project his company had financed and he'd wanted her there.

She had become addicted to his texts. Usually a curt two lines telling her where and when he needed her to be. She'd travelled all over the globe in the last two months. To Rio, to Cannes, to Paris and Hong Kong and even Niagara Falls. Whenever he'd summoned her, she'd gone. She'd become an expert at smiling for the cameras, and addicted to the stolen hours they had alone together, before and after the balls and galas, the charity banquets and high-profile sporting events he needed his wife to be seen at.

They spoke often about her growing business.

His advice and encouragement had proved invaluable and he seemed genuinely interested in her progress.

But the wall he had erected after the almost-collapse of their marriage remained. It had cost her not to try to breach that wall again, to talk about more than just sex or business, because the yearning to know him better, to understand every little thing about him, remained too. He fascinated her, he always had and that would never change. But she'd forced herself to be content with the companionship—and the spectacular sex—and to remember the deal they'd made. That this relationship had a sell-by date—a sell-by date she'd agreed to.

Plus she adored being with him, and she didn't want to ruin their time together with pointless yearning for something more, when she already had so much.

Just as it was pointless to wish she could get his advice about this latest disaster. He always had a solution, and was willing to share his phenomenal expertise—but she didn't see how he could help her with this.

She was an upstart, a newbie, in this business. She'd wanted to succeed, not just for herself, but also to repay him for his confidence in her. But renting a studio in Holborn, hiring a business manager and a personal assistant and a brilliant seamstress, didn't suddenly make her a fashion designer. What it made her was a fraud—no wonder Rohana hadn't wanted her beautiful fabrics gracing the Allycat Collection.

Ally closed the back door and dumped her bag on the hall stand.

She rubbed her belly, the dull ache from the period that had started that morning just one more thing to drag her spirits down into her boots.

She slipped off the wet shoes, and took a moment to knead her arches, which were sore after twelve hours spent on her feet directing traffic at the studio.

As she stood in the hallway where they'd first met again all those weeks ago, another wave of melancholy blindsided her.

Dominic had never returned to their London home… *Her* London home. Since that first night and the following morning.

She totally understood that. His life, his work, was in New York.

But as she stood staring into the empty hallway, she missed him. Terribly. Why not admit it? She missed him a little bit more every time she had to fly back to London without him.

How wonderful would it be to have him here tonight? To have that broad shoulder to lean on. That glorious body to explore, so she didn't have to think about how she was going to drag herself back up after this latest knock-down.

She tried to shake off the loneliness and longing, as she had so many times before, and headed towards the kitchen.

Get over yourself, Jones. You're just knackered. And scared.

As she approached the kitchen she picked up the muted hum of the TV playing a news channel.

She stopped. Hesitated.

Had Charlotte, the housekeeper, left the set on? Before she'd left for the evening?

Edging open the kitchen door, she gasped. 'Dominic?'

The wave of emotion almost floored her.

Was she having an out-of-body experience? Because she'd imagined him in her home, *their* home, so many times in the last couple of months? Had she somehow conjured him up because she needed him here?

He seemed real and solid enough though, as he turned from the countertop. Dressed in faded denim and a T-shirt, his feet bare and his hair mussed, he looked so different from how she usually saw him—which was either formally dressed or gloriously naked.

'At last you're home. Where have you been?' he said, in his usual direct way, the slight frown making her heart tick into her throat. 'It's past ten o'clock—you should have finished work hours ago.'

Yup, that was her husband: pushy and over-protective.

He stalked towards her, then cradled her cheek, his gaze gliding over her face, his expression intense and observant. *'Tu as l'air fatiguée.'*

You look exhausted.

She leaned into his callused palm despite the less than complimentary comment. Joy enveloped her as she breathed in his scent. Spicy cologne and clean pine soap. A scent she often dreamed about on the nights she spent alone.

She covered his hand. 'I didn't know you

were coming to London,' she said, not making any effort to keep the pleasure out of her voice. 'It's so wonderful to see you.'

She smothered the tiny voice, warning her not to get sentimental, or over-invested. Just this once, she wanted to rejoice in the unexpected gift of spending an evening home alone with her husband.

'I've got a meeting in Mayfair tomorrow,' he said. 'And some news about the business that I wanted to deliver in person.'

News? About his business? She couldn't imagine what it could be, but it was so good to have him standing in front of her, warm and solid and frowning. And even more wonderful to know that when something happened in his working life, she was the one he wanted to tell about it.

It was comforting to know that even if their marriage had considerable limitations they had managed to become friends as well as lovers in the last two months.

'What's the news?' she said, then grimaced as a cramp tightened across her abdomen.

He swore softly, then clasped her shoulders. 'What's wrong? Are you ill?'

'No, I'm… I'm fine,' she said, stupidly pleased by his concern.

'Don't lie,' he said, lifting her chin. 'I can see the pain in your eyes.'

'It's nothing,' she said, but the cramp chose that precise moment to tighten like a vice and a small groan escaped her lips.

'That's it!' He tugged his smartphone out of his back pocket. 'I'm calling an ambulance.'

She laughed and grasped his wrist as he lifted the phone to his ear. 'Dominic, don't. Really, that's not necessary, it's just…' She hesitated, a flush heating her skin.

'It's just what?' he demanded, his frown deepening.

'It's period pain,' she said, realising how ridiculous it was to be embarrassed to talk to her husband about something so natural. 'It started this morning. It's always sore the first twelve hours or so.'

His arm dropped, as he tucked the phone back into his pocket, but the frown remained. She wondered if he was one of those men who freaked out about women's menstrual cycles. Weird she didn't even know that, when they'd been married for two months. But then being on the pill meant she'd been able to time her periods so they didn't fall on the nights they spent together.

'Have you taken any painkillers?' He slid a warm hand around her neck, his thumb stroking the pulse-point below her ear.

'Not yet,' she said.

He pressed a kiss to her forehead. 'Then let's fix that, first,' he said with his usual confidence.

No surprise there, then. Dominic *wasn't* one of those guys who was freaked out by periods. But then why would he be? He'd dated loads of women before her.

She stifled the ungenerous thought. And the prickle of envy that came with it. He was with *her* now, in *their* kitchen. That was what mattered.

Crossing to the kitchen counter, he opened and closed the drawers.

'They're in the drawer on the far right,' she said, realising she had moved things around some since he'd lived here.

He poured her a glass of water and watched while she took a pill. Then handed her another.

'Take two,' he said. 'I didn't like the sound of that groan.'

She dutifully obeyed then handed him back the glass.

'Is there anything else that will help?' he asked. 'A massage? A heat pack? Food? Wine? Sex?'

'*Sex?* You wish!' She smiled at the urgent, solicitous tone. 'That's the absolute last thing I want,' she said, protesting maybe a bit too much as a familiar heat flushed her skin.

Who knew? The thought of making love to her husband while she was having her period wasn't nearly as icky as she might once have assumed. But he didn't need to know that, she decided. It would be nice just to absorb him tonight and the novelty of having him in their home, and take some much-needed comfort from their friendship to bolster her flagging ego. Her period was the perfect excuse not to jump each other the first chance they got.

'Well, hey, it was worth a try,' he said, smiling sheepishly as he put the box of pills and the water glass on the countertop.

Nope, definitely not a guy freaked out by periods.

'So what's your news?' she said, trying to get comfortable on the kitchen stool as her belly tightened again. 'Is it the Waterfront deal?'

'Nope,' he said. 'But I'm not telling you until we've got you comfortable. I don't want you freaking out on me.'

Freaking out? Why would she freak out? Her tired mind shot straight to a worst-case scenario. Was he about to tell her he didn't need his fake wife any more?

'*Arrêtes*... Stop it.' His smile widened as he clasped her chin. 'I can see you're panicking already. Relax, it's good news, I swear. You're going to be pleased when you get used to the idea.'

Get used to the idea. Okay, that didn't sound that good either. How could something to do with his business affect her, other than their marriage? But then he kissed her on the nose, the gesture so sweet, her heart butted her tonsils so hard she had trouble breathing, let alone thinking.

Dominic forced himself to release her, aware of the emotion glittering in her eyes. And ignored the tight feeling in his chest.

He'd dealt with this feeling many times before. His heart felt too full, too big every time he gave her advice and her eyes lit up with understanding, every time he gave her a compliment and she blushed, every time they made love and he watched her respond without holding an ounce of herself back until she shattered. And every time he left her bed and the desire to keep her, to hold her, to stay with her just a little longer threatened to overwhelm him.

This time was no different from any of those. He couldn't allow himself to get sentimental about what they had, or too attached.

It would only complicate this relationship more. And it was already complicated enough. But as she looked at him, the gratitude plain on her face, he couldn't seem to make himself regret his concern at the bruised smudges under her eyes. She needed a decent meal, and for the painkillers to kick in before he told her his news.

He knew it was going to freak her out, because according to Megan she'd already resisted this development, which was why he'd flown across an ocean to persuade her.

That was her insecurity talking. She needed

a nudge now, and he intended to give it to her. But only once she'd stopped looking so fragile.

The sweet smile, and the explanation—that she was struggling with period pain—had been a relief. So much so that when her smile had disappeared, he'd felt the loss of it right down to his soul.

And he had a bad feeling he knew the cause. She had assumed he was going to suggest they end the marriage.

Which was insane. Why would he end an arrangement that was working so well?

He'd been in complete control of when and where and how often they met. And the sex had been phenomenal—hot, raw and wildly exciting. So much so that he'd got into the habit of accepting invitations to events he would never usually have bothered attending—simply so he would have an excuse to get his hands on her hot, sweet, responsive body again.

Which had to explain why each time they were together, each time he took her to his bed, he'd found it harder and harder not to demand she stay.

It was probably a good thing she was on her

period and not in the mood this evening. He needed to put a few brakes on his libido.

Too much of a good thing was turning him into a fool.

'Have you eaten?' he asked. 'It should get the painkillers working faster.'

'Not since breakfast.'

He swore under his breath. 'No wonder you look so pale.'

He returned to the counter where he'd begun to assemble a sandwich from the supplies he'd found in the fridge.

'What do you want on your sandwich?' he asked. 'There's three different types of ham, Emmental and provolone cheese, *de la salade*, *des avocats et des tomates*?'

'Anything and everything,' she said and he glanced over his shoulder. 'I'm starving.'

'What's so funny?' he asked, even though her spontaneous smile had tugged on the weight in his chest.

She propped herself back on the stool, the flush of pleasure on her cheeks only making her more captivating. 'I'm just looking forward to sitting here and watching the big bad billionaire make me a sandwich.'

He raised an eyebrow at the amused and incredulous tone. 'You think I don't know how to make a sandwich? I worked twelve-hour shifts making sandwiches in a bistro on the Ile de France for six weeks after busting my ankle on the bike the summer after I arrived in Paris.'

'You broke your ankle?' Her face fell comically. 'How? Were you badly hurt?'

The concern shadowing her eyes had the weight in his chest dropping down into his stomach. Not good. 'Long story,' he murmured.

She got the message and didn't press, and the moment passed. Thankfully.

They ate their sandwiches with a Cabernet he had found in the cellar. And she asked him about four more times to tell her his news. He resisted, until he had her resting in the living room on the sofa. Sitting beside her, he picked up her feet and put them in his lap, because the urge to touch her never went away, period or no period.

She sighed, and a deep shudder went through her as he dug into the arch of her foot with his thumb.

'Good?' he asked, pleased as he felt the tight

muscle release—even if her soft moan wasn't making him feel particularly relaxed.

'Spectacular,' she murmured, the flushed smile the only reward he needed.

'How is the pain?'

'Gone,' she said. 'Now will you tell me what your business news is?'

He assessed her to make sure she wasn't lying, but she looked comfortable and sated, and as relaxed as he was going to get her.

He worked the muscles in her feet a moment more. Realising he was a little nervous himself. He had been sure this was a good thing, that she needed this push, but he hoped he hadn't miscalculated.

'Dominic, please,' she said. 'What's happening with your business?'

'It's not my business, it's yours. Or rather ours.'

'What about it?' she said, her foot tensing right back up again.

'I've arranged for you to show the Allycat Collection at a Fashion Week prelim event for new designers in July in TriBeCa. Megan suggested it. It's basically a competition to win a spot at the week itself in September.'

'You did what?' She jerked her feet out of his lap, her face going so pale she looked as if she were about to pass out. 'You can't be serious? I'm not ready for this. The collection's not ready. July is only a few weeks away.'

'It's a month and a half away,' he said.

'Oh, God.' She swung her feet to the floor and bent over, clutching her stomach as if she were about to be sick. 'I haven't even made any of the prototypes yet,' she moaned.

'Megan told me the designs are incredible and the make-up and fitting stage shouldn't take more than a month. Plus you only need a small sample for this show.'

'You've been talking to Megan behind my back?' She was still clutching her stomach, the horrified expression making the weight in his abdomen swell.

He'd known she would be against the idea at first, which was precisely why he'd taken this step without consulting her. She was still letting her insecurities rule her decision-making process.

'Megan only brought the opportunity up in passing because she couldn't understand why you hadn't thought of entering. I contacted the organisers on my own.'

'You don't know what you've done.' She stood up, pressing a hand to her forehead. 'Maybe I could back out.'

He stood and placed his hands on her shoulders, turned her round to face him. 'We're not backing out,' he said. 'Whatever you need to make this happen, you have my full support.'

He hadn't meant to upset her and it made his stomach hurt too, to see her in this much distress; he hadn't realised she was still this insecure. Everything she'd told him about the business, and everything he'd gleaned from Megan, had been overwhelmingly positive. Apparently, she'd been holding out on him.

But that didn't alter the fact this was a great opportunity. Even if she didn't win the competition, it would give her visibility and experience. So far, she'd stayed in her comfort zone. You couldn't make things happen in business if you did that.

'I can't do it,' she said, the panic and devastation clear in her voice. 'I don't even have the proper materials any more. The fabric I had planned to use as the signature feature of my collection just got poached by another designer.'

He held her shoulders and pulled her into his arms. Damn, she was shaking. She wasn't just freaking out now, she was having a full-on panic attack.

He cradled her face in his hands, pulled her gaze to his. 'Can you get a replacement?'

'It took me two months to find this one. And I don't have that time. Not if I'm going to show a collection that doesn't even exist in six weeks.'

At least she was admitting the show would happen. He took that as a positive step.

Reaching into his back pocket, he pulled out his phone. 'Who's the supplier?'

'It's a Mumbai co-operative. They work with girls and women who have been abused or made homeless. Their workmanship is exquisite and the fabrics they make stunning. But they need exposure, exposure I can't give them. It was naïve of me to think I could when I'm…'

'This show will give them exposure, no?'

'Yes, but…' Flags of colour appeared on her pale cheeks, but her eyes remained dark with fear. 'Not the exposure they need, if it's a disaster.'

His frustration flared—why hadn't she told him about this problem when she'd arrived? But he banked it. She was scared. He understood scared. But he had her back. That was what he'd promised her two months ago. Now it was time to deliver.

'What's the name of the co-operative?' he asked.

'The Dharavi Collective.'

He keyed in Selene Hartley's number and lifted the phone to his ear. 'Selene, there is a fabric workshop in Mumbai called the Dharavi Collective. Allycat Designs would like to secure exclusive use of their fabrics for the next year. We will beat any price they have been offered by a rival brand and would also like to put the full weight of LN India behind them to get funding and exposure for their charitable work.'

After Selene had asked him a few further questions about the negotiation, he ended the call.

'If they have already signed with your rivals we can negotiate with them for a licence to use the material.'

Alison blinked, looking shell-shocked. 'I didn't know you had offices in India.'

'LeGrand Nationale is an international company,' he said. 'I've been to India many times. It's a fascinating, beautiful country, full of talent and initiative. And projects such as this collective. Why wouldn't I have offices there?'

'Yes, why wouldn't you?' she said. But her chin dropped to her chest and her shoulders slumped and he knew they were not out of the woods yet.

The fabric situation was only a symptom of a much bigger roadblock. Alison's fear of failure.

He tucked a knuckle under her chin. 'You must talk to me, Alison. I can't help, if you don't tell me what the problem is.'

'I just…' She sighed. 'I'm not sure I'm good enough. Everything's happening too fast. I'm scared to make a mistake, to let anyone down. If the show fails, the—'

'No, no, no.' He gripped her face, pressed a kiss to her forehead, to stop the rambling irrational fears. 'This is nonsense, Alison.' The heavy weight twisted into a knot. 'You won't fail, but, even if you did, it is not the end, it is just an opportunity. A beginning. There are many ways we can ensure the collective will be okay, but that's not the real fear that is holding you back, am I right?'

She sucked in a jerky breath, and he watched her step back from the cliff edge, but then she nodded. Because however panicked she was, she was not stupid.

'Yes, the real fear is that I'll fail. That I'll take everyone down with me. But I don't know how to stop worrying about it. How to get past it.'

'You never stop worrying, that's not how it works,' he said. 'I have over five thousand employees worldwide. People who depend on me to feed and clothe and house themselves and their families. And that responsibility weighs on me constantly. But every day I take new risks. Sometimes there is a reward, other times a punishment. And if the risk doesn't pay off, if I fail, I try to bear the brunt of the punishment, to protect the people who work for me. But without the risk and the reward, my business would die anyway, do you see?'

'But it's easier for you to take those risks,' she said, although he could see he was getting through, because the colour had come back into her cheeks. 'You're good at it. You know when a risk is worth taking and how to survive the punishment.'

'Precisely, so next time you must let me help. Not bottle up your fear.'

His phone buzzed. He pulled it out of his pocket and read the text from Selene. Then smiled.

Problem solved.

Clicking on the link Selene had sent through, he passed the phone to his wife. 'Your new fabric supplier Rohana has a message for you.'

He watched over Alison's shoulder as the message played. An excited woman, gesticulating madly at the screen, told Alison how pleased they were to be working with her on the collection and how they couldn't wait to send the first batch of materials.

Alison sniffed as she passed him back the phone. 'I don't believe it. You fixed a problem I've been wrestling with for weeks in a two-minute phone call.' Her grin was tentative but there, which was all he cared about. They had weathered this storm, just like the last one. She would do the show, despite her misgivings, and it would be a triumph, because just like the

Dharavi Collective she was brilliant at what she did, even if she was the last one to believe it.

He nodded. 'Of course.'

She choked out a laugh. 'I guess being married to a twenty-eight-year-old billionaire has it uses,' she said. 'Even if I keep tripping over his enormous ego.'

He laughed. Slinging an arm around her shoulder, he placed a kiss on the top of her head, to resist the powerful urge to kiss the teasing smile off her lips. Because that would be bound to start something they would not be able to finish.

'Actually I'm not that precocious,' he murmured. 'I turned twenty-nine while we were in Paris.'

He only realised his mistake when she whipped round and stared at him, her eyes huge with shock.

'It was your birthday while we were in Paris? Why didn't you say something? We should have celebrated. I should have bought you a present. Baked you a cake. Something. Perhaps we could celebrate it now?'

The weight in his stomach twisted back into

a knot as he noticed the sheen of hope and excitement.

'Forget I mentioned it,' he said. 'I don't celebrate it,' he added.

'Why not?' she said.

'Because I never have,' he replied.

'*Never?* Not even when you were a child?' She sounded horrified.

'My mother didn't consider my birth something to celebrate,' he said. 'Getting pregnant was what ended her affair with my father.'

He'd always tried not to let it bother him. Marking his birthday each year would have been painful for his mother. It had made him feel left out when other children had talked about their birthdays, but he'd forced himself not to care. They hadn't had money for gifts anyway, so what would have been the point? In truth, he'd only found out about his birth date by accident, after discovering his birth certificate—with his father's name on it—in one of his mother's drawers.

'But, Dominic, that's awful.'

'What you don't have, you don't miss,' he said, suddenly wanting to cut off the conversation. Why had he confided so much?

'Are you sure you don't want to start celebrating it?' Alison said. 'I make a mean chocolate cake.'

'Yes, I'm sure.'

He steeled himself against the shadow of hurt in her eyes. And the brutal pang of longing. What would be the point of celebrating his birthday this year, when there would be no one here to celebrate with him next year?

CHAPTER ELEVEN

Can you come to Rome tomorrow night? Se-lene will make all the arrangements if you can spare the time before the show. D

ALLY READ THE text that had popped up on her smartphone five minutes ago for the twentieth time. Or was it the thirtieth time? She was looking for hidden meaning, or additional information. Or some sign that things had changed in their relationship, if only a little bit, since their night together in London.

But Dominic's text was exactly the same as all the others she'd received over the past three months requesting her presence by his side—polite, pragmatic and distant.

The giddy jump in her pulse was familiar, but the strange feeling of disappointment not so much.

Why had she expected there to be something more this time? It had been three whole weeks since his visit to London—and they had both been extremely busy.

Three weeks since she'd woken up to find him gone again, and had been stupidly crestfallen.

They'd had a wonderful evening, after he'd given her a heart-to-heart about her business, persuaded her to do the runway show in TriBeCa and fixed her problem with the Dharavi Collection...

And confided in her why he didn't celebrate his birthday.

But as they'd sat on the couch together watching an old black and white movie on the large flat-screen TV she never used, a series of unanswered questions had tormented her. How had he survived as a child with so little love? How selfish was his mother, that she hadn't wanted to celebrate her son's birth? Had she made him feel guilty just for being born? It had made Ally feel desperately sad for him. But it had made her even sadder to know he didn't want to celebrate it with her.

He'd shut down as soon as he'd told her, closed himself off again and made it clear she couldn't go there. So she hadn't.

Still she'd hoped he might be there in the morning. So she could get up the guts to ask him a few of the questions that still burned inside her, but of course he hadn't been.

She clicked on the phone's reply bar but her fingers stalled as she tried to formulate a response to the businesslike text—a reply that didn't sound too needy, or too clingy, or too over-emotional.

This was an invitation she'd been waiting for and hoping to receive every day for the past three weeks, ever since that morning—she didn't want to spoil it with expectations that were unlikely to be fulfilled.

Eventually she settled on a simple reply.

Looking forward to it. I could do with a break from all the chaos here. A

But as soon as she'd sent the text, she added another line.

I've never been to Rome.

She didn't want him to know how much she was looking forward to seeing him.

What mattered wasn't what Dominic put in a

text, but that he had asked her to be with him and she was going to see him again, tomorrow night.

Twenty-four hours later she was feeling considerably less positive as she stood in the empty penthouse suite of a five-star hotel overlooking the Palazzo Poli.

Decorated in glorious Baroque flourishes to match the building outside, with an imposing four-poster bed in the main bedchamber, the suite of rooms was spectacular. She'd been whisked by limousine from Fiumicino airport and then greeted in Dominic's suite two hours ago by one of his assistants and a small army of beauty professionals. Ally had brought her own gown for the evening—one of the early prototypes she and her seamstress had been working on for the past two weeks. But even after being prepped by the team of beauticians and a hair stylist for an hour, she didn't feel any more secure.

Why hadn't Dominic met her at the airport? It was nearly six o'clock and she'd been ready for over an hour; all she'd received so far was a text to say he would be late—but no explanation as to why.

Rome's nightlife buzzed with vitality a hundred feet below as she stood on the suite's ornate balcony. The scene was awe-inspiring—or should have been. The water tumbled over the iconic Roman stonework of the Trevi Fountain, given an enchanting glow by the nightlights. The fountain was the imposing centrepiece of a square choked with tourists and a few courting couples.

But, unlike the many other new sights and sounds she'd seen since marrying Dominic, the scene below her failed to inspire the usual excitement or exhilaration. Because, for the first time, he wasn't here to share it with her.

Her gaze landed on one of the couples in the square, fooling around on the side of the fountain. The girl stood with her back to the water and threw in a coin over her shoulder. Her boyfriend locked his arms round her waist and swung her in a circle. The noise of the crowd and the free-flowing water drowned out the sound but she was sure she could hear the girl's carefree giggle floating on the warm Roman evening.

The sight pierced her heart—reminding her of the time when Dominic had lifted her and spun her around in his arms when they'd agreed to become business partners. She'd felt so young and happy in that moment, convinced that, whatever the limitations of their marriage, she was doing the right thing, but now she wasn't so sure. Had she become too dependent on Dominic, on his strength and support? She'd tried so hard to remember that end-date, that this relationship was essentially a business arrangement with some spectacular benefits. But why didn't it feel like that any more? And where had this yearning come from to know more about him, to have him give her more?

She heard the suite door open and close behind her.

A low voice rippled down her spine. 'Alison, *bonsoir*—sorry I am late.'

Swinging round, she felt her heart leap into her throat. The swell of emotion so strong and elemental at the sight of him—strong and indomitable in the tailored tuxedo—it flooded through her body like a tsunami.

And suddenly she knew the answer to the

question she had been so careful not to ask herself until now.

The reason she wanted more, she needed more, was that she had fallen hopelessly in love with her husband.

'Bonsoir,' she said, her voice coming out on a panicked whisper as she pressed shaking palms into the red velvet of her gown.

Oh, Ally, what have you done?

'You look exquisite,' he murmured.

She forced a smile to her lips, despite her fear. 'So do you.'

In a tuxedo Dominic was completely devastating. But that wasn't the reason her heartrate was accelerating like a racing car on the starting grid at Brands Hatch.

He gripped her fingers and pulled her into his embrace. Something dark and dangerous flared in his rich chocolate eyes and he pressed his lips to her neck, making the sensitive skin sizzle and burn.

'I wish we didn't have to go to this damn event now,' he murmured as his hands stroked her bottom.

She felt the instinctive shudder of need—and wished they didn't have to attend it either.

Her panties were already damp at the prospect of his lovemaking. She wanted the security of hard, sweaty sex, of feeling him deep inside her, to take the fear and panic away. At least for a little while. Until she knew what to do with this revelation. Because she instinctively knew Dominic was far from ready to hear it.

But surely he would be, given time. He'd already been like a real husband in so many respects, offering her support and encouragement, pushing her to be the best she could be in business. Giving her ecstasy and security in equal measure. And she hoped she'd given him the same. If only he would let her give him her love this could be a good marriage, a strong marriage, a lasting one.

'Do we have to go?' she asked.

He let out a strained chuckle and lifted his head. 'Unfortunately, yes. It is a charity event. If we do not show it will reflect very badly on our public image.' He smiled, the sensual smile that always drove her wild—full of a boyish charm she had come to adore. 'Especially as everyone will guess what we were doing instead.'

She blushed as his teasing ignited the hot spot between her thighs.

'Plus we don't want to waste an opportunity for you to get exposure for this dress.' His hand remained fastened to her side as he led her across the suite to pick up the stole she'd left on the chaise longue. 'Is it one of the designs for the show?'

He wrapped the stole around her bare shoulders and then lifted the tendrils of hair that hung down her neck.

'Yes,' she said, hearing the strained chuckle at her shiver of reaction.

'It is beautiful,' he said, the desire flaring in his eyes as he escorted her to the penthouse suite's private elevator.

She held onto him as they stepped into the gilded lift. The fear and panic coalescing in her stomach into a wellspring of hope as he murmured: 'You are going to be a sensation in three weeks' time.'

And for the first time, she believed it. If she could conquer that fear, surely she could conquer this one, too, and find a way to tell him, eventually, how much more she wanted from this marriage.

* * *

They arrived at the elegant forecourt of the Teatro dell'Opera di Roma less than fifteen minutes later for a production of Verdi's *Otello*.

Ally absorbed the stunning grandeur of the nineteenth-century auditorium as they were escorted into the royal box—red velvet upholstery and curtains added another layer of luxury to the intricate gold plasterwork. She dipped her head back, letting her gaze travel past the five tiers of viewing galleries at the other side of the stage until it reached the rotunda decorated with nymphs and cherubs cavorting across a heavenly sky.

While Dominic thanked the young usher who had brought them to their seats and gave him a generous tip, Ally scanned the programme. She didn't understand much of it because it was all written in Italian, until her gaze snagged on the name of the charity, which was in French. How odd. *Fondation pour les Garçons Perdus.*

'That's interesting,' she said as Dominic took the seat beside her. 'The charity this event is supporting is French.'

'Is it?' he said, undoing the button on his tuxedo, but tension had rippled across his jaw.

'I think so. The name is French. Doesn't that mean Foundation for Lost Boys?' She showed him the programme, pointing to the French wording.

'Yes, I guess so,' he said, but then he took the programme from her hand and placed it on the table in front of them. 'Come here,' he said, and gripped her hand as the lights dimmed.

'Dominic, what are you doing?' she gasped as he tugged her out of her seat.

As applause rained down from the different tiers, the opening bars of the opera rang around the auditorium—stark and dramatic—and the curtain lifted, she found herself pulled into Dominic's lap. His callused palm sent giddy arousal sinking into her sex as it stroked her thigh under her gown.

'I want you too much,' he growled as his hand sank into her hair, sending the pins holding the elaborate do flying.

Before she could protest, or even get her bearings, his mouth was on hers—firm, seeking, demanding. His tongue drove the hunger as he forced her to straddle him, her damp panties connecting with the thick ridge in his pants.

He was fully erect, hard and long. The feel of

his need was like a match lighting the fire inside her. As he sucked on her tongue, drawing her deeper into the erotic fog, his hand travelled to the juncture of her thighs and the heel of his palm pressed against the aching bundle of nerves.

She bucked, the contact too sweet, too brutal.

'Dominic?' She dragged her head back. 'We can't, we'll be arrested. People can see us.' She moaned against his ear as his hand continued to tantalise the swelling spot between her legs. The music and the deep male voices from the stage reached a crescendo, drowning out her ragged pants as the battle raged inside her.

'No one is watching,' he said, the urgency in his voice matching her own.

But even cocooned in darkness, she felt exposed, raw, her heart sinking into her abdomen, her need too visceral, too demanding.

'Stand up,' he commanded, then grasped her waist to lift her off his lap. He stood and dragged her to the side of the booth, giving them a semblance of privacy, hidden behind the heavy velvet curtain she'd been admiring only moments before.

'I want to be inside you,' he said.

She nodded, her heart ramming her throat at the urgency in his voice.

She could have sworn she could hear the sibilant hum of his zip releasing above the cacophony of sound coming from the stage. His hands stole under the layers of velvet and taffeta in her dress; her back butted the wall as he boosted her into his arms.

'Wrap your legs around my waist,' he urged, the thick head of his penis probing past the gusset of her panties and finding the slick folds of her yearning sex.

She did as he told her, disorientated. How could she survive this need? This desperation?

She clung to him as he thrust heavily inside her.

She groaned, the fullness immense. He paused, but only for a moment, to give her time to adjust to the brutal pleasure. Then he started to move. Slow at first, but then faster, harder, rocking out, thrusting deep. Her pants became sobs, his groans became grunts, until all she could hear, all she could feel was the devastating wave washing through her like a tsunami. She tumbled over, but he didn't stop, didn't even slow down, dragging her back into the maelstrom.

The dark need grew again, becoming huge, becoming overwhelming, the coil at her core twisting, as he dug ruthlessly at the spot inside her he knew would destroy her control... The pleasure became pain, so sharp, too sharp. She clung on, grasping his shoulders, and rode the whirlwind only he could create.

'*Encore.*'

The guttural French demand echoed in her head.

Again.

She plunged over the edge, her cry muffled against his shoulder as he plunged into her one last time and then followed.

Her galloping heartbeat slowed, but her wits remained scattered in the heady wave of afterglow. His fingers tensed on her hips, the ache immense as he eased out of her.

He held her arm as she tried to steady herself, her legs like limp noodles, as he placed her on her feet.

She must look a mess, her dress creased, her breathing uneven, her hair falling down on one side.

'Pardon,' he said, the word so rigid and filled with self-disgust she flinched. 'I don't know what happened to me.'

She lifted a hand to his cheek, caressed his stiff jaw, hearing the self-recriminations, the fury with himself, and wanted to weep. 'It's okay, Dominic, I was desperate, too. It's been a long three weeks.'

And I love you.

The declaration echoed in her mind, but she held onto the words. It was too soon, not the right moment, to burden him with more, when he already seemed to be burdened with so much she didn't understand.

His phone buzzed. He lifted it out of his pocket and she could see the screen.

A woman's face appeared by the call sign, next to the name 'Marlena'.

Who's Marlena?

'I must take this,' he said, then stepped away from her.

He spoke furiously into the phone in a stream of fluent Italian.

He spoke Italian?

Whoever Marlena was, she had his full attention as the call continued, none of which she understood.

It could only have lasted a few minutes, but it felt like hours as she watched the emotions cross his face in the shadows of the booth, for once unguarded and unrestrained. Concern, panic, desperation, was that what his love really looked like?

Desdemona's melodic soprano from the stage couldn't drown out the discordant beats of her heart as he ended the call.

'I must leave,' he said.

He lifted her fingers to buzz a kiss across the knuckles but his detachment, his distance, felt like a physical blow. He wasn't here with her any more, he was with Marlena.

'Wait, Dominic.' She held onto his hand, refusing to let him discard her so easily when her sex was still aching from his lovemaking.

She knew he'd kept things from her. She knew he had never wanted her to see past the barriers he put around his heart. And she'd respected that because she'd thought she had to, until he was ready. Until they were *both* ready to take the next step.

But she had never thought, not even for a moment, that this marriage had been a complete sham—a cover for something else.

All this time, while she had been convinced he wasn't ready to love, had he been giving what she yearned for to someone else?

'Who's Marlena?' she asked, her voice dull.

His scarred brow rose in surprise, but then she saw the guilt flicker across his face.

'She does not concern you,' he said. 'Stay and enjoy the rest of the show.' The suggestion came out as a command. Cold and final.

As he strode out of the box without a backward glance, her heart—which had been so full, so joyous, so hopeful only moments before—shattered.

Dominic was still shaking as he climbed into the SUV and barked an instruction at his driver.

A new message appeared on his phone in Italian from Marlena Romano.

Dominic, there is no need to leave the event. We have alerted the police to Enzo's disappearance and will inform you as soon as we have any news.

He typed a reply in Italian—not easy with his fingers still trembling from the feel of his wife, coming apart in his arms. And the look of devastation on her face afterwards.

Not a problem, Marlena. I am on my way.

He had caught Enzo, a ten-year-old street kid, trying to pick his pocket that afternoon, while he had been waiting outside the hotel for the car that was due to take him to the airport and Alison.

He'd been so preoccupied with thoughts of his wife and how much he wanted to see her again, to hold her, to find out how her show was progressing, that the nimble-fingered young thief had almost got away with his wallet.

But as soon as he'd grabbed the child's bony wrist, heard the boy's cry of distress and seen the angry defiance in his jaded eyes, it had been like looking into a mirror. And all the reasons why he shouldn't be quite so eager to see Alison again had come tumbling back to him.

Marlena was right, of course. It wasn't an efficient use of his celebrity to leave an event that had been planned for months to help fund the

Lost Boys charity he had set up in Rome and a collection of other European cities, to help street kids like himself, both boys and girls—children who had no hope and no chance and no opportunities. To give them the support and encouragement they needed to succeed and tap all that wasted talent and potential before it was too late.

All he would be doing was getting in the way. Marlena and her staff were highly trained and extremely capable and once the police located Enzo, and returned him, the staff would be better placed to convince the boy to take the chance the home could offer him.

But when he had received Marlena's call he hadn't been thinking straight. The truth was he hadn't been thinking at all.

He'd needed a way out, an excuse to escape from the emotions threatening to choke him as he'd looked at his wife's dishevelled appearance, and the dazed shock in her eyes, and felt like an animal.

How could his hunger, his need, have got so spectacularly out of control that he'd taken her against a wall during a public event? When was it ever going to end? Because the more he had her, the more wild he became.

And the driving hunger for sex wasn't even the worst of how delusional he was.

He'd seen the way Alison had gazed at him when he strode into the hotel suite earlier that evening. Her eyes soft with longing.

They only had a few more months of their marriage left, and already he had let it get so far out of hand he couldn't even control his hunger for her, let alone the greed to have more of her than he could ever deserve.

That would have to end tonight. He would speak to Marlena, gauge the situation with Enzo, wait for word from the police and stay away from Alison until she had gone back to London. And he wouldn't contact her again, until he was finally back in control of his senses.

The car sped past the Coliseum on its way out of Rome towards the suburbs.

The arc lights illuminated the ancient building's broken façade and for the first time, instead of seeing the epic majesty of the place, and everything the people who had built it had achieved, all he saw was a ruin, the brutal bloodshed once celebrated within its walls a symbol of the hollow shame inside him.

CHAPTER TWELVE

ALLY WATCHED THE black SUV stop in front of a large mansion block in the outskirts of the city.

Dominic got out of the car and headed past the children's play equipment in the building's front garden, the bars of a climbing frame glinting in the moonlight. Confusion accelerated the hammer thuds of her heartbeat.

She wasn't even sure what had possessed her to follow him. She'd left the opera in a daze, the pain of his betrayal so huge it was almost choking her.

The questions running through her mind telling her what a fool she'd been.

Why had she assumed their marriage would be exclusive? After all, he'd never put that stipulation in any of the paperwork he'd made her sign. Why had it never even occurred to her to ask? Because she'd never asked him about anything? She'd never insisted or demanded a single thing. She'd trusted him implicitly, right from the first.

But as the young cab driver had sped through the streets of Rome following the SUV with the skill and precision of Jason Bourne in a chase scene—and telling her in broken English how much he'd always wanted a fare like this one—the open wound in her chest had made it brutally clear that stupidity and naiveté weren't her only flaws. She still loved him, despite her suspicions.

'*Scusa, signorina?* You go in?' the cab driver asked from the front of the car.

Did she want to go in? Indecision added to the trauma.

The building Dominic had disappeared into looked like a school. Or maybe a children's home.

Did his mistress work here? What if she'd made a terrible mistake and he wasn't seeing another woman? Perhaps she should return to the hotel as he'd requested, wait for him to come back?

But even as the desperate hope that she had been wrong, or misguided, that she'd jumped to the wrong conclusion, bubbled inside her, the voice in her head that had persuaded her to follow him in the first place refused to be silent.

Was this really about whether or not Dominic had been seeing another woman? Or was it much more fundamental than that?

He'd shut her out, from so much of his life, his past, his future, and yet he had become such an important part of hers. He'd refused to let her in. Hidden behind the business arrangement they'd made long after it had stopped being just about business and become so much more for her.

She'd fallen in love with him weeks ago, maybe even months ago, and she'd been in denial about that, too. But she wasn't in denial any more.

Whatever this place was, whoever Marlena was, they were significant in Dominic's life and yet she knew nothing about them. Good grief, she hadn't even known her husband spoke fluent Italian.

He'd talked about trust once before, when they'd consolidated their marriage bargain—but she'd always trusted him. It was him who had never trusted her...

Opening her purse with trembling fingers,

she pulled out two twenty-euro notes and passed them to the driver. *'Grazie, mille.'*

'Grazie, signorina. You want I wait?' he asked as he took the money.

Yes. Just in case I don't get up the guts to follow him into that building.

She stifled the plea. She'd been enough of a coward already. Letting him set the boundaries of this relationship. She didn't want to be bound by that contract any more. She wanted a real marriage. Or no marriage at all. She couldn't live like this, or she would be exactly what she'd always strived to avoid. A shadow of who she could be, a woman like her mother, chasing dreams and not facing reality.

'No, *grazie,'* she said and forced herself to step out of the car.

She took a deep breath, which did nothing to calm her racing heartbeat, or close the hole that had opened up in her belly. And walked up the path to the building's main entrance as the cab drove away.

As she rang the bell she read the sign on the door: *Fondazione per Ragazzi Perduti.*

It was an Italian translation of the charity

named in the opera programme—the charity Dominic had pretended to know nothing about.

The bitter truth stabbed at her stomach like a rusty blade. So he'd lied about that too.

The door opened, and a middle-aged woman in jeans and a jumper stood in front of her, her warm caramel eyes widening in surprise.

Marlena.

Ally recognised her immediately; she was striking, even though she looked considerably older than she had in the picture on Dominic's phone Ally had glimpsed a half-hour ago.

Ally almost smiled at the shock on the woman's face. This situation would have been comical if it weren't so tragic.

'Signora LeGrand?' she said, and Ally realised she must have recognised her from the press photos, but as Ally nodded, unable to speak round the boulder of misery in her throat, the woman didn't look remotely guilty or abashed.

A tiny portion of the pain faded. So Marlena wasn't Dominic's lover. She had been wrong about that. But the relief she ought to have felt didn't come.

Why had Dominic deliberately let her assume the worst? Exactly how much contempt did he have for her and their marriage? And how much more pathetic could he make her feel? When she had chased him across Rome simply to have the truth confirmed.

'Buena sera,' the woman said, her expression changing from surprise to concern. 'Come,' she said, gesturing for Ally to step into the lobby of the building. 'Dominic is here—you are looking for him, yes?'

The lobby was warm and bright, modern and colourful. Framed children's paintings covered the walls. There was a chalkboard pinned with a series of flyers and messages in Italian. She could hear rap music playing and see what looked like a rec room through a glass partition, where a group of teenagers lounged, some watching a football game on a large flatscreen TV, others competing with each other on a computer console.

'I told him he did not need to come,' Marlena said from behind her, her English perfect. 'Enzo absconded earlier, but the police have found him. I am so sorry your evening has been interrupted.'

'Enzo? Who's Enzo?' she said, blankly.

'Enzo is the homeless boy Dominic caught trying to pick his pocket this afternoon.' The woman smiled, but her puzzled expression said it all; clearly she had expected Dominic to mention this boy to Ally.

'Dominic brought him to us earlier. He is one of the many children Dominic has helped with his patronage of *la fondazione*,' the woman added.

Her explanation was drowned out by the pounding in Ally's ears when Dominic appeared from a door at the back of the lobby, staring at his phone as he spoke in a stream of Italian. The only word she understood was *'polizia'*.

'Dominic?' Marlena interrupted him and his head jerked up. 'Your wife has arrived.'

His whole body stiffened, and Ally felt the rusty blade in her stomach twist.

'Alison, why are you here?' he said, the edge in his voice sharpening the knife. She wasn't wanted here, in this part of his life, that much was obvious.

'I... I came to find you,' she managed to get out as he marched towards her.

'Come.' His fingers closed over her bare arm

like an iron band. 'We should leave.' He said his goodbyes to Marlena, but didn't give her a chance to do the same before he had escorted her out of the building.

'Get in the car,' he said as he opened the door to the large black SUV.

She slid into the seat, and stared out of the window as she heard him get in behind her. Her stomach felt as if it were a ship in a storm, being tossed on the undulating waves of her emotions. She couldn't speak, couldn't even think as the car pulled away from the kerb.

'I cannot believe you followed me here,' he said, sounding both angry and incredulous. 'When I asked you to stay at the opera.'

She ought to say something, in her own defence, but as she gazed into the night she decided for once she had nothing to apologise for. If he hadn't wanted her there, he shouldn't have left her with the impression he was running off to see another woman.

'I'd appreciate it if you didn't do that again.' He bit off the words in staccato bursts of temper. 'I prefer not to be humiliated in front of people who work for me.'

Wouldn't we all prefer that? she thought bitterly.

Silence descended over the dark interior of the car as they made their way back through the city. The tension became like a living breathing thing as she refused to look at him. But finally the one thing that had always failed her in the past began to burn in her gullet like a comet, choking off everything else—the heartache, the pain, the humiliation, the embarrassment, the confusion and panic—until all that was left was the rage.

The rage that she had learned to bury deep, during the years spent watching her mother die.

The car pulled up at the kerb, but, instead of waiting for Dominic to get out and walk around the car to open her door, Ally got out on her own and marched towards the hotel entrance.

She heard him shout something behind her, but she kept on going, the rage cleansing, empowering, enlightening. It flowed through her veins now, burning through everything in its wake like a fireball.

He caught up with her in the lobby, grasped her arm to swing her round to face him. 'Where the hell do you think you are going?' he said—looking wary now as well as angry.

Good.

'To our suite, to pack my bag and go home.' She yanked her elbow free.

Everything she could say, everything she wanted to say, everything she should have said weeks, maybe even months ago careered around her head like dodgem cars in a cheap arcade as she stormed into the elevator and stabbed the button. She'd left him standing in the lobby. He shook his head, as if he were dazed, and then charged after her, but he was too late, the doors closing before he could get his hand inside.

'*Arrêtes*, Alison, we must talk,' he shouted, obviously expecting her to hit the 'open door' button. She didn't.

Everything that needed to be said was still lodged in her solar plexus.

The elevator arrived at their floor. She scrambled in her purse to find the key card, desperate to get into the suite and lock him out.

He'd broken her heart deliberately. It was the only thing her tired brain could grasp hold of. He'd known how she was coming to feel about him, and he'd hurt her, crushed her because he could.

She found the card, but as the green light flashed on the door, the emergency exit slammed open. He must have run up the stairs rather than waiting for the elevator. His footsteps raced down the corridor.

She rushed inside, swung round to slam the door closed just as his palm slapped against the wood. He pushed it open and she scrambled back into the room.

'Get out. I don't want you in here,' she said, the tears streaking down her face.

'*Ma belle*, stop—don't cry...you mustn't cry.'

He reached out to cradle her cheek, his anger replaced by devastation.

But she slapped his hand away. 'Why mustn't I?' she said around the choking sobs now.

'Because I am not worth it,' he said.

Did he really believe that? It seemed that he did from the shame and regret burning in his eyes. But she didn't care, she wasn't going to let him off that easily.

'Why did you do it? Why did you let me believe Marlena was your mistress? Why won't you let me into your life? Why does everything have to be a secret?'

'Because you would hate me more, if you knew what was inside here.'

He pressed a hand to his heart, the need and desire in his eyes almost as painful as the shame.

She backed up until there was nowhere else to go.

'Let me love you. Let me take away the pain?' he said.

He was talking about sex, she understood that, when she wanted so much more, but she couldn't say no to him as he found the zip on the back of her dress and pulled it down. She pushed his jacket off his shoulders, yanked at the buttons on his shirt; the fight to get naked became a battle.

He kicked off his shoes, she unhooked her bra, he unzipped his trousers, shoved them down, the rampant erection bouncing up to tempt her, to mock her.

Within seconds they were naked, panting, the feral need to mate, to forget, gripping them both the way it had in the opera booth. He turned her to the wall, spread her legs and placed his palm above her head as he notched the thick head of penis at her entrance and thrust in from behind.

The visceral wave of pleasure as he ground into her stole her breath and her resistance and the whole of her heart.

Their frantic mating was over in seconds, the glorious peak slamming into her with the force and fury of a freight train as he emptied himself inside her for the second time that night.

They sank to the carpet together, their breathing ragged, the sweat drying on their skin. But as she turned in his arms, to hold his head, to look into his eyes—they hadn't settled anything, they'd only made it more complicated—her gaze snagged on the cheval mirror at the other side of the room. At first all she saw was the tangle of limbs, her pale skin starkly white against his tanned body. Then her heart seized.

A criss-cross of white scars marred the smooth skin of his back. The marks ranged from his shoulder blades right down to the lighter skin of his backside.

What had happened to him? Who could have done such a thing?

'Some people deserve to be hurt, ma petite.'

And suddenly she knew exactly who. And the

words he had whispered before they'd fallen on each other—to try and erase the hurt with sex—came back, too.

'Because I am not worth it.'

Sharp pain dug into her stomach, her gasp of distress ringing off the room's luxury furnishings.

His body went rigid and he heaved himself off her. Their gazes locked.

Shame flickered across his face, making the knife in her gut plunge deeper.

All the questions, came tumbling back, but she had answers to them all now.

So this was why they'd always made love in the dark or the semi-darkness…why he always left her in the morning…why he hadn't shared a bedroom with her…why he locked the door so she couldn't join him in the bathroom. It was another secret he'd guarded for three months.

He reached behind him to drag on the shirt that had fallen off his shoulder. To cover the scars.

She grasped his wrist, felt the warm blood pulsing through him, and her heart broke inside for the boy he'd been. 'Don't hide them from me, Dominic, you don't need to,' she whispered, naked, vulnerable, but unafraid.

She'd had no idea his father had been such a monster, but how could she not have known, when all the signs had always been there?

'Your back… The scars…' She choked the words out and saw the muscle in his cheek flex as he looked away. 'Did Pierre do that?'

His eyes darkened, his expression becoming strained and tense.

'I'm so sorry.' She allowed all the compassion she felt for that boy to show in her face.

'Why are you sorry? You didn't do it,' he said, his voice clipped and wary. 'It was a long time ago and I deserved it.'

'Dominic, how can you possibly believe that?'

Dominic pressed his thumb to her lips. He didn't want to talk about that time in his life, or that night. Why the heck did she think he'd gone to so much trouble to stop her seeing the scars? But he hated seeing the sheen of moisture in her eyes, the compassion he didn't deserve.

Somehow, she had sneaked under his skin. Made him care when he didn't want to care.

Made him want more than he should. And more than he would ever be able to reciprocate.

She was so young and vulnerable, so honest and open, so brave and strong, but she had no idea who he really was. He had hoped to keep this from her, had clung to the delusion that if she never discovered the truth, they could end their marriage with dignity. But this relationship had never played out on the terms he'd tried to insist upon. He'd become captivated, enchanted by her and invested in a future he had no right to expect.

And by trying to protect her he'd only hurt her more.

'I'm not that screwed-up kid any more, and my father has been dead for a long time,' he said, determined to take that misty look out of her eyes.

'I know, but why did you hide…?'

'Shh, Alison.' He stroked his thumb across her lips—wishing he could kiss her into silence. But knowing he had to stop being a coward, and tell her the truth.

She blinked, those amber eyes glossy with tears. 'Did you get those scars that night? Because you were protecting my mother?'

'No.' If only that were true. 'She was protecting me, that's why he hit her, why he threw
you both out. I snapped, sick of the insults. I
thought I could best him, thought I could finally make him pay for what he'd done to my
mother, by abandoning her and me. But I was
wrong. I was a stupid child, hyped up on my
own bitterness and resentment. She found him
using his belt on me and she tried to stop him.'

'Oh, Dominic…' Her eyes widened, the compassion so fierce, he had to fist his fingers to
stop from taking what he wanted from her. 'I'm
so sorry…'

'You misunderstand me, Alison. I was young
and foolish and full of bravado and I was spoil-
ing for a fight with him. And you and your
mother paid the price.'

'You can't blame yourself for your father's
violence, surely you must see that,' she said.
'You didn't do anything wrong.'

Hadn't he? It certainly hadn't felt right when
he had been crawling through the grounds,
puking into the underbrush as he'd struggled
to breathe through three broken ribs and stave
off unconsciousness before he got to the road.

'Maybe.' He wanted to believe the faith in

her eyes; he'd lived with the guilt of that night ever since he'd found out how destitute she and her mother had been. But that wasn't the biggest problem. 'The point is I'm not that boy any more. I look after number one now. Always. I can't give you what you need.'

He brushed her short curls back from her cheek, pressed his lips to the soft skin. She shuddered with reaction, her wide amber eyes darkening on cue.

He forced himself to drop his hand, the rough chuckle strained.

'Yes, you can. You already have. I love you, Dominic,' she said, with such yearning, such honesty. 'So much.'

The guilt gripped his insides.

This was his own fault. He'd stepped over a line three weeks ago in London, maybe even before that. Every time they made love, he wanted to absorb more of her kindness, her care, her tenderness—and Alison's romantic nature, her sweet, compassionate heart had done the rest.

'You can't love me,' he said, forcing his voice to remain firm, despite the riot of emotions churning in his stomach. 'You don't know me.'

He found his boxers and put them on. Then handed her his shirt and turned his back, waiting for her to cover herself. He threaded his fingers through his hair, his hand shaking. He couldn't look at her, couldn't see the pale skin, the marks he'd left on it from their lovemaking, and tell her the truth.

'You cannot love me, Allycat,' he said, his voice breaking on the words. 'No one can.'

'Why not?' Ally asked.

Dominic lifted his head, his chocolate eyes full of the secrets that he'd worked so hard to hide. And suddenly she understood, who he had been protecting all this time—with his insistence on them living separate lives, in separate countries. Why he had never wanted to stay overnight, why he had hidden the scars, denied their significance, even denied her feelings for him.

He hadn't been protecting himself, he had been protecting her.

'Why, Dominic?' she asked again. 'Why can't I love you?'

He shook his head, looked past her, but the light had left his eyes, becoming flat and wary.

'I am sorry I hurt you,' he said with a finality that chilled her. 'That was not my intention, even if it was inevitable. I will have my lawyers finalise the divorce.'

But as he turned to go, to walk out of her life, she rushed after him and grasped his arm.

'Dominic, stop.'

He glanced down at her fingers, but she refused to remove them. She curled her hand around his forearm instead and gathered every ounce of her courage to say the one thing she knew he would not want to hear. The one thing he had denied for so long, the thing that had been inculcated in him as a young boy by a woman who had never wanted to celebrate his birth and a man who had acknowledged him on a whim one summer and then discarded him in the cruellest way imaginable.

'You're not worthless,' she said.

He tugged his arm free, the amused frown a defence.

'I know I'm not. LN is worth upwards of five billion dollars on the open market,' he said.

'You're not worthless,' she said again.

'I know that,' he replied. But he backed up a step, and her heart broke for him all over again.

The arrogance, the control, the desperate need not to accept her love. Not to need it. It had all been a defence, all along. Because he'd loved his mother and tried to gain his father's respect and they had both thrown his need back in his face.

Of course he didn't trust her feelings, because he didn't trust his own.

This marriage *had* always been more than a business arrangement. His desire to cherish and protect her. His insistence that he invest in her business. His encouragement and concern. And she'd let her own insecurities blind her to that truth. She hadn't challenged him…she hadn't even put up a fight. But she was going to fight now.

'You're not worthless,' she said again. 'Whatever she made you think, whatever he told you. You're not.'

He shook his head, but she could see the arrogance falling away. She'd struck right at the heart of his insecurities but she couldn't let up now. However painful it was for him, however big a risk it was for her, she had to see this through.

'I *do* love you. And it's not because you're

incredible in bed, or one of the richest guys on the planet. Or because you've supported my business, supported me.' She let out a weak laugh as the confused frown descended on his face.

No one had ever loved him for who he was. But she did. And she intended for him to know it and believe it. Then they would see.

'Why, then?' he asked, as if he genuinely didn't know. And she had the opening she needed.

'It's because you let me follow you around like a puppy that summer and you never once complained. It's because you blamed yourself for what happened to my mother, to me, when it was never your fault.'

'But you suffered so much,' he said.

'And so did you,' she said, realising so much of that valiant boy—who had wanted payback for his own mother and had taken on a monster to do it—still existed, even if he couldn't see it. 'It's because when I rang your bell all those months ago, you insisted on tending my leg.'

'I was planning to seduce you,' he qualified again. 'I needed a wife.'

She grinned. 'Do you hear me complaining?'

'You were innocent,' he said, his eyes dark with the heat and intensity she had come to adore. 'However much you enjoyed it,' he added, cupping her cheek.

She felt the sizzle of heat, and the connection that had always been there, ever since that summer, arc between them.

She covered his hand, leant into the caress. 'I loved that you were so scared of exploiting that innocence, even though it really wasn't a big deal to me,' she said, loving his concerned frown even more.

Honestly, men! What was the big deal with virginity?

'And because you fought to give me security and stability in this marriage,' she added, the swelling in her chest making her heart beat in hard, heavy thuds. 'Even though it was supposed to be fake.'

'It never felt fake, even when I wanted it to,' he murmured, cupping her other cheek, and touching her forehead with his.

At last, she'd broken through that shield he erected to protect himself from rejection. The shield that had made him believe he didn't deserve to be loved. That he didn't deserve her.

The connection was so sure, so solid, she could hear it in his ragged breathing. How ridiculous that they'd both denied the importance of that connection for so long.

'It's because you're the kind of man who wants to give children like Enzo the helping hand you never had,' she continued. 'And because you pulled out all the stops to help me achieve my dream, even when I was busy sabotaging it with self-doubt.' She sighed. 'And because you gave me a foot rub to try and ease my pain.'

'That's such a small thing,' he murmured, his voice barely a whisper as she held his waist and he caressed her neck, his fingers threading into her hair.

'Well, it was a really excellent foot rub,' she said, smiling at him. 'So not *that* small.' Then she sobered. 'It's the small things that matter, Dominic. As much as, if not more than, the big things.' She drew back, so she could look into his eyes. The small things they'd both been denied by living separate lives when they deserved to be together.

'Now do you believe I love you?' she asked quietly.

He nodded. 'But do you love me enough to stay with me?' he asked, the yearning, the longing that she'd thought was hers alone clear in his voice.

She sucked in a deep breath. Knowing it would be so easy to just say yes. She already had so much more than she'd thought she'd have. But she couldn't chicken out. Her cowardice—and his—had brought them to this point. Now they both needed to be brave. He'd been brave enough to admit how unsure he was about love. She needed to be brave enough to demand what she needed.

'I want to stay, but I have conditions.'

His eyebrow arched. 'Conditions? What kind of conditions? Are we going to have to renegotiate the contract again?'

She laughed, the breath releasing in a rush. Maybe this was going to be much easier than she had assumed. 'No, we're going to have to tear it up.'

'I see,' he said.

'I don't want a time limit on our marriage. I want... I want us to be a real couple in every sense of the word. I don't want to limit my feelings for you. And I want us to live together.

Either in London or New York, or wherever works.'

He nodded. 'I'm sure we can work something out,' he said, and her heart leapt into her throat.

'I want to be able to tell you I love you. And know that it doesn't scare you, or threaten you or—'

'It doesn't,' he said, interrupting her. 'It humbles me.'

'Really?' she asked, letting the last of her insecurities show.

'*Dieu*, Alison. How could it not?' he said. He stroked her cheek. 'You're so tough and smart and sweet. How could I not fall in love with you?'

'You don't have to say that to make me stay, Dominic,' she said, wanting to take the words at face value, but knowing she couldn't. Hadn't her mother believed them for all the wrong reasons? At least she wasn't going to make that mistake. 'Love is a gift, not an obligation,' she said, because she suspected he had no idea what love was. Who had ever loved him, but her? 'It's enough that you want to give this relationship a chance. A real chance. You don't have to love me back. Not yet.'

'That's very generous of you,' he said, but his lips curved in a rueful smile and she felt the bubble of hope break open inside her chest, spreading warmth and light where only minutes ago there had been despair. 'Unfortunately, it's too late for that,' he whispered against her lips, the soft glow of happiness joined by the sharp pulse of heat. 'Because I already do.'

Dominic let his mouth take hers, claiming his wife in a kiss that touched his very soul. He was still scared, still terrified really. He wasn't convinced he was as worthy as she believed him to be. Was still sure he didn't deserve her. But after almost losing her, he was damned if he would let that hold him back from claiming her ever again.

She was his wife now, in every sense of the word. Damn the contract, damn his father, damn the fear that had held him back from admitting how he really felt for so long.

Yes, it was a huge risk. But Alison Jones, his Cinderella bride, was worth every ounce of effort it was going to take for him to prove, to himself as much as her, that he deserved to be her husband.

EPILOGUE

Fifteen months later

'SOCIAL MEDIA IS going mad, Ally. And listen to that applause. It's another triumph for the Allycat brand.' Megan De Rossi gave Ally a high-five as the last model strutted onto the catwalk and the wave of noise hit the backstage area. 'Consider New York Fashion Week well and truly conquered,' Megan added, tears forming in her eyes. 'You did it—they adore you.'

'*We* did it,' Ally said, beaming back at her. 'They adore *us*.'

All the hard work, the long hours, the endless worries about everything from a model's sprained ankle yesterday to those first days over a year ago when Dominic had secured her partnership with the Dharavi Collective had paid off. It had been a long hard road to this point—and there would be more bumps along the way—but her brand was due to launch at the end of the month in Europe at Paris Fashion Week and she was already clothing A-list movie stars, Grammy-winning pop stars and a string of influential celebrity vloggers. And now this, another triumph in TriBeCa after that nail-biting baptism of fire a year ago now, when she'd done that first prelim show Dominic had pushed her into.

She could still remember the sweat and tears of that first shaky step onto the fashion industry's world stage. Her nerves had reached fever pitch that evening but she'd pushed through them, and Dominic had been beside her at every step. Offering not just support and encouragement, but also his strength and determination. And the rewards had been immense, not just in that first tentative triumph—although she hadn't won a spot at New York Fashion Week that year, the exposure had started a word-of-mouth buzz about her designs that had led to orders and other opportunities—but also inside herself. Because after that night, she'd discovered that Dominic was right, that risk in business was the same as the risk she'd taken in her private life on him, on them… That risk wasn't something to be afraid of, not if you embraced it and put your all into it, because with risk came rewards, rewards beyond her wildest dreams.

'Come on, you need to take a bow,' Rohana, who was here with some of the women from her collective, shouted above the applause as she and Megan linked arms with Ally to lead her onto the catwalk.

As her team roared their support from the wings, she walked down the narrow runway with the two women who had been an integral part of making her brand such a success.

The cheers reached epic proportions, camera phones flashing, the media spotlights trained on her as the crowd rose to their feet.

But as she waved, and smiled, and bowed, she scanned the crowd. She could see Dario, Megan's husband, standing in the front row with their daughter Issy—who had been given special dispensation to attend the show without her brothers—and Katie, Megan's sister, with her husband, Jared, who had their toddler daughter, Carmen, in his arms. But where was Dominic? She needed him here, because this was his triumph as much as hers.

'Be still my beating heart,' whispered Rohana. 'Your man is a fine sight to see.'

It was all the warning she had before Dominic leapt up on stage.

He strode towards her—the dark blue business suit doing nothing to disguise the ripple of muscle in his big body. The crowd went wild, beginning a chant of 'Kiss her' as he approached—which had become a feature of all her shows since that sidewalk kiss all those months ago in Nolita had made them an Internet sensation.

How far we've come, she thought as he reached her. Gripping her round the waist, he swung her round in a circle, then put her down and cradled her face in his palms.

'Congratulations, Allycat,' he said, then his lips were on hers. The kiss was driven, hungry, joyous, igniting all the needs that would never die.

Her hands found his waist as she clung to him and kissed him back, her tongue tangling with his, and let the love pour through her.

This man, this marriage, meant everything to her. Without it, without him, without love, even wowing New York Fashion Week wouldn't mean as much.

* * *

It was several hours later before they were finally alone together, in the limousine heading back to their Manhattan apartment. The apartment they rarely used since Dominic had made the decision to move permanently to London.

Ally clung to his hand, wishing she could just be beamed up now to their bedroom and they could finally celebrate the brand's latest success in style.

'Happy?' he murmured as he pressed her fingers to his lips.

'Ecstatic,' she said.

'*Bien*, because I have a suggestion,' he said.

'What is it?' she asked, loving the mischievous glint in his eyes. She certainly hoped his suggestion involved them both getting naked as soon as possible.

But then he surprised her.

'That we both take the next week off. It is way past time we had a honeymoon. Can you do it?' he asked.

'Absolutely,' she said without hesitation, because she couldn't think of anything more wonderful. It would mean rearranging her schedule, postponing the interviews she had lined up, getting her team to handle the European launch, but they'd already done a ton of advance publicity, and she trusted them.

'Where would you like to go?' he said. 'Name anywhere in the world and I will take you.'

'Honestly? I can choose anywhere?' she said, knowing there was only one place she wanted to go. And one person she wanted to be with.

Over the past year, her wanderlust had been sated a hundred times over. Ever since that night in Rome, when they had committed to making this a real marriage, life had been a roller coaster as she'd set up her business and his had continued to expand. They'd worked overtime to make this marriage work but it had meant shoehorning snippets of quality time in between all their other commitments. Each moment they'd spent alone together had been precious and wonderful and important...

But a whole week felt like a banquet, a banquet she didn't want to squander on sightseeing, or shopping, or elaborate meals in fancy hotels.

'Of course,' he said. 'Wherever you want to go, it is your choice.'

'Okay, then I want to go home to London, shut the doors, turn off our phones and the Internet, tell everyone we've gone to Outer Mongolia and just stay there, with you, for a week. I want us to watch slushy movies together, cook all our favourite foods, have sex in every room and finally get around to celebrating all the birthdays of yours that we've missed.'

They'd celebrated his thirtieth birthday that summer and the memory of the particularly inventive way he'd found to devour the chocolate cake she'd baked him still made her blush.

Even so, she held her breath, wondering if he would object. Dominic was an active, driven over-achiever; getting him to sit still for long was never easy. But instead of objecting, he threw back his head and laughed. The sound was deep, and sexy and—was that relief she could hear?

Reaching across the seat to cup her cheek and pull her towards him, he whispered across her mouth. 'I like your thinking, Madame Le-Grand. But I'm not sure we have enough bedrooms—there are twenty-nine birthdays to catch up on, after all.' Running a hand under her dress, he found the melting heart of her. 'But do not worry,' he added as his mouth descended to seal the deal. 'I can improvise.'

Happiness burst like a firework in her chest—not least because she knew exactly how good her husband was at improvising.

* * * * *

LET'S TALK
Romance

For exclusive extracts, competitions
and special offers, find us online:

- f facebook.com/millsandboon
- 📷 @millsandboonuk
- 🐦 @millsandboon

Or get in touch on 0844 844 1351*

For all the latest titles coming soon,
visit millsandboon.co.uk/nextmonth